THE HANGMAN'S GAME

ALSO BY Karen King-Aribisala

Our Wife and Other Stories
Kicking Tongues

ACKNOWLEDGEMENTS

All of my writings are dedicated to God and *The Hangman's Game* is no exception.

I thank my friends at the Mac Dowell Colony, Peterborough, especially G.C. Waldrep III for his immeasurable support; Soon Mi Yoo, Maggie Dubris and Mimi Schwartz, all of whom helped me to realize this work.

Special thanks also to my dear friends Benedicte Le Dent for her constant 'nagging'; to Elise Johnston for her fierce critiques; to Bolaji for crying when she typed some of the manuscript; to my agent Donald Gibson who 'believes' in me; to my godfather and uncle Alex Miller who godfathers and uncles me like no one else.

I thank my dad Kenneth King for loving me to extremity and for his encouragement and my late mother Joyce who read the manuscript and pronounced 'good success' on it.

Lastly I thank my two Femi Aribisalas, my husband and my son for their ready love and Karen-commitment.

K.A.K.A.

KAREN KING-ARIBISALA

THE HANGMAN'S GAME

PEEPAL TREE

First published in Great Britain in 2007, reprinted 2008
Peepal Tree Press
17 King's Avenue
Leeds LS6 1QS
England

ISBN 13: 9781845230463

ARTS COUNCIL
ENGLAND   Peepal Tree gratefully acknowledges Arts Council support

PART ONE

BLIND

They wanted me dead. I don't mean physical death. I'm not afraid of that any more. Once you're dead you go to heaven or hell. It's that simple. The death they wanted for me was spiritual – I think that's what I mean – to have me beset by fears, doubts; the insecurities of action and word that take their toll and make you live a life of death.

I was coming under their influence, allowing them to dominate my life and my thoughts – which, in one sense is as it should be if you're in the process of creating lives, a time, a place. But they were hanging me with a rope of my own making, squeezing the life out of me in wretchedly subservient gasps. What was maddening was that I was the one giving them the power to do it. It began with my obsession with that absurd children's game of Hangman. The game goes like this: you draw a pole onto a blank sheet of paper, then you draw a bar on the pole so that it looks like a reversed seven. Not the Genesis-creation-positive seven, but seven the wrong way round – a destructive seven. At the bottom of the pole you draw a square, so that the hanging structure can stand solid. Then you and your opponent begin the word play. One draws in dashes for the letters of a word they have in their mind. If you guess a letter right, it's written on the appropriate dash. Should you guess wrong, the hanging begins; your opponent starts to draw a line from which the roundness of an O springs; that's the head of the hanging man. More wrong guesses and a long down-drawn line represents the body – awaiting the sticks of arms and legs; two arms, two legs, two feet connected to a body along with a neck attached to a head. Add that up and you've got seven body appendages until you're hanged.

They were playing with me, with my words, inviting me to a hanging death. All seven of them in their devious innocent ways.

7

There was Mary rattling away in her half-demented nursery-rhyme, fairy-tale style; an Englishwoman, beautiful, longing to gain control of her life and her husband, and plotting against him and me to gain it. Rosita, with her childish, pretty-pretty ways and her wanting a husband not hers, was no better – Rosita of the flower-like, up-turned gaze which she turned on John Smithers, husband of Mary. There was John, the missionary, so desirous of bringing black souls to God. This was his life's purpose and he let everyone know it; in his resolve so like Quamina of the squat, purposeful bow-legs with his passionate desire for freedom that churned him up and caught him in a dream of death for life. Then there was the Governor, with his damning creed of the inconsequence of black lives (denying the dense, matt-black of his mistress, Auntie Lou – and her thumping of the big black book and her mice and poison). And finally, Captain (or Dr.) McTurkeyen with his gruff insensitivity, his righteous slave-catching handlebar whiskers.

All of them – Mary, Rosita, John, the Governor, Quamina and Auntie Lou and Captain McTurkeyen – wanted me dead, and would have gotten away with it if I hadn't been able to control their words, their thoughts and actions. Had I not done so I would have been dead, hanged by the neck in their hangman's game.

The cheek of it! To create and nourish them, and then they, in a "body", attempt to "do me in". Their time was another century, it is true. The nineteenth century to be exact.

Mary's husband, John Smithers, was appointed by the London Missionary Society. Off they went to Guyana, South America, in those days called British Guiana; more particularly they went to Demerara, the place where the sugar cane is grown. Slavery still existed. (As a matter of fact, slavery of various sorts is still there.) Though the sale and transport of black slaves from Africa to the so-called New World was no longer going on (some Britishers like Wilberforce and Canning had voiced loud indignation at this bartering of human flesh) slavery itself had not yet ended. My Governor, of the murderous seven, vehemently opposed the efforts of his fellow Britons in England and stifled the news of the coming emancipation. He wanted to remain absolute Governor; slavery was a just institution; the blacks were black were black. He cosseted these notions along with a tight colonial knot of buckra plantation owners, who, having what they wanted, created a web of deceit and terror to keep it. This did not prevent the slaves from revolting in what was the last slave insurrection in Demerara in 1823. Buildings were set on fire and razed to the ground. Whites were murdered in their beds and as they walked. Slaves were executed. Blood ran. The militia was brought in to restore order and a curfew imposed on the colony. But it was the last slave revolt. The emancipation of slaves became a reality. I am that reality. Yes, I am that reality or illusion. Call it what you will. Or perhaps I should say, "Yea, I am that reality."

As real as the day when, under a hot noonscape of blue sky, I left my house and drove past Smith's Church, close beside Quamina Square, past his statue, eyes defiant in stone; parked and climbed the twentieth-century steps of the Nigerian Embassy in Georgetown. Knock knock. It was the only African embassy in the country so I thought I'd try them. I wanted, desperately, to understand the reasons behind our ancestral enslavement. What better way than to get a visa to Nigeria, a country that had trafficked in slaves, and live among its peoples and discover at first hand why hands exchanged silver for the likes of me?

Books – fiction, history or political treatise – could not tell the whole story, if indeed there was a whole story to tell. The door was answered by a man in a loose, tent-like affair which, I later learnt, is called an agbada. He ushered me into a waiting room. I filled out forms and I was interviewed by a gaunt, bespectacled woman, the frames sliding off her nose because the day was so hot and the sweat trickled and her face was shiny and moist with it.

"So you want to go and live in Nigeria?" she asked, perusing the forms.

"Yea."

She looked up. "Yea?"

"I mean yes. I want to go there on vacation. I mean, I'm actually doing research on a novel… for a novel on Reverend John Smith and the 1823 slave revolt…"

"Don't you have any information at the University of Guyana?"

"Yes. I've got a photocopy of the trial of Smith and some other stuff about slavery in the region. I've also been to England... on a grant..."

"I don't think I quite understand your reason for wanting to go to Nigeria. You're not one of those on the Back to Africa bandwagon are you?"

What if I was? But she was smiling gently and had given up the sweaty battle with her spectacles. Her eyes, I saw, were large and clear.

"I want to see for myself why slavery, the slave trade, occurred in the first place." I took the plunge. "I want to know why blacks sold their fellow blacks into slavery and I want to know why God allowed it."

"We did not sell our fellow blacks, as you say, into slavery." She held the spectacles by one of their arms and swung them round. I watched the movement, annoyed with myself for having divulged so much to a stranger. Now, because of my rash words, I wouldn't get to Nigeria. She stared at me.

"I'm going to be unconventional here. You have the funds to stay in Nigeria, and for your flight ticket, yes..." Her fingers skimmed through my documents. Suddenly she looked up again.

"Why did you say yea?"

"Why?"

"Yea why?" She laughed and I relaxed.

"Because I've been trying to read the King James version of the Bible and somehow I've been thinking and talking in that language, that story I mean..."

"I see. Spiritual are we? And Christian?... Don't bother to answer, I'll say 'yea' for both of us." We laughed.

"Would you like something to drink?"

I nodded, and over iced lemonade we talked. She had been living in Georgetown for about six months. She thought the place charming but too rural and dead. She hailed from Lagos and spoke wistfully of its intoxicating bustle, people, colour and business continually on the move. I was given the visa. Now all that remained was to pack my luggage, my writing materials, my books and of course my Bible. I was on my way with those seven characters in my head, ready to write and to see my thoughts come alive on paper. Only on the paper, you must understand. Only on the paper with my words.

★ ★ ★ ★ ★

The flight was long. I stopped over in London for a few hours and then Lagos, Nigeria was before me.

Murtala Muhammed Airport in Lagos. Hot bustle. Electricity and fans at a standstill. Dead. Queues mopping at streaming sweat. Backs and armpits; dark circles. Airport officials shouting. My contact, a university professor, is there to meet me with a curiously dry handshake. Yes, the journey was tiring. I'm fine. Thank you. Only one piece of luggage? It's the books that's making it so heavy. Thank you for the arrangements you've made for my stay; the people you've arranged to meet me.

I can't think with this strange scenario, which was mine once, and is now so real and definite it hurts my mind. The land everywhere is bright orange. It is hard. Palm trees nod gracefully. The roads are wide and so is the sky. It is on a sky-widened road that we are periodically stopped by soldiers. My companion says this is for our safety. A strange safety patrolled by guns and bayonets, I think. One "safety" asks me for one of my books, or foreign exchange.

Questions. The road again. This time we are caught up in a winding line of vehicles which, my companion says, is called "Go Slow" in local parlance. The time edges past and it is hot. We open the car window and turn off the gas. We need to save petrol. My companion is apologetic but snoozes. It will be a long wait. I need to do something. I nudge him and ask if he is interested in playing the Hangman's Game.

"The what?" He says the game sounds macabre but at least it's a word game. His field is semantics and he readily complies. He is also a lay pastor. The Word and the word. We play and I win. He gets bored. We are near the soldiers who have been holding up the queue. More questions. What are you doing in Nigeria? I hope your writing will be favourable? We are all blacks. We should help each other for the sake of the race, should we not?

A skirmish and booted soldier legs are kicking a man who is

11

screaming. He's a traitor. A smuggler. People like him are unpatriotic. They give Nigeria a bad name. My companion is profuse with his apologies. Is Guyana any better? Eighteenth, nineteenth or twentieth century, I ask him? Is anywhere any better? He seems relieved, especially when I bring out my Bible and start reading. I find it difficult to read, to understand. I'm still near the beginning and it's the Egyptians enslaving the Israelites. So what's new? I feel him touch my hand and in that touch I feel his caring and his love and we have only just met. In this short (and long) ride from the airport to the guest house, he falls in love with me and I with him and I don't know how or why. We spend a month in each other's company, day in, day out. Talking. And in his talking and in his words, spirit-filled, I know I have met the bone of my bone and the flesh of my flesh. In one month I know this. I love my man among men beyond anything and he loves me. We are like a married couple who have known each other through the passing years. I can tell him the worst about me and be mind-naked with all my faults up front. When the darkness of the Hangman's Game comes, my characters encircling me, putting me on edge, making me doubt, he does not condemn me to the death of a life without him loving me. He accepts me as I am and perceives the good in me that will come. He embraces me, the real me and the unreal me, as is. Covenant committed in law, in flesh, in spirit; he would die for me. We are married before we are married. Still, he proposes and we are married in a simple way at the registry office on Kingsway Road, with some disinterested goats outside, chewing. They have eaten most of the shrubs in the area and are fat – as fat as my stomach became with our first child, a beautiful little girl.

For a time, life continues and my book does not. The characters, the seven, follow me around peopling my thoughts with so much business. But they are in their own world and I am in mine. So I think. But not for long. Very soon I am pregnant again. A two-year gap between children is healthy the doctors say.

So I am in a healthy two-year gap. What could be better than that? But increasingly, the seven dog me with their lives and I know that they all want me dead: Mary, Rosita, John, the Governor (Theophilus Murrain), Quamina, Aunty Lou, Captain McTurkeyen want to place a rope around my neck, which is still

12

a slim neck unthickened by the years, and they want to string me up and pull the rope tight and taut and see my legs dangle, dance, then stop. Their stories I birthed with my own words. Now this. My own implant implanting. Plantocracy. Word. Slavery. Word. Christianity. Word. Words?

I had used these thought-laden words in a semblance of historical fact, creating fiction out of facts. And now – to think of it! To think that I intended to document the horror of slavery's wasted life and blood and those seven have leapt out of the pages of the historical papers I was reading. (Shortly I intend to buy some actual paper to start my own writing.) To think that they want to enslave me as they have been enslaved, bespeak their wretched lives into my life and turn my world into a chaos of time! It maddens my blood. I will have none of it. My own day of insurrection has come. They will not take me out of control of my self. My words are my words, not their words which they can use to weapon me out of existence. They are only characters that, in all innocence, I created. It is true that I read an account of Rev. John Smith, nicknamed the Demerara Martyr, of how he tried to bring the Demerara slaves to Christ and was caught up in the slave revolt of 1823, charged with treason, convicted and sentenced to hang for his efforts. That had made me mad. It was so unjust. But I had used only the bones of this historical account for my own story. The plot was mine but my characters were intent on out-plotting me. As God is my witness, I was going to be in control whether they liked it or not – or kill them off. Mary, with her nursery-rhyme rantings, her wish to dominate her husband and thereby gain control over herself, was not me. Her husband, John, was not my husband. He would never be so preoccupied with his mission as to leave me so alone that I would plan revenge. Rosita would get her come-uppance by the time I had finished with her. Perhaps a slow death with that rope of long black hair before she goes too far. As for the others – the Governor of Demerara and Auntie Lou, his not-so-faithful servant, his mistress who plotted and planned with my very own plots and plans, and the devilish McTurkeyen – I'd get them down on paper where I wanted them. Pat. Especially the Governor. Quamina I might leave alone. I feel an uneasy sympathy for him. Indeed, in

13

a way, the seven are all my children, deviant as they are. I must be firm. I must make them do what I want. I must not be blind as to what will happen if I do not control them. My time is the twentieth century. Their place is a mind place. My characters, my plots, are under my pen and shall be seen to be so, especially by those seven, who have tried to suck me into a labyrinth, a long winding maze of insecurities.

When did my anger begin? When did I first become conscious of them dragging me in? I had been struggling for days to find the opening line of my novel and then, out of the blue, it came when I attended a funeral.

I don't usually go to funerals. I don't like the wailing. Once you're dead, you're dead. I used to be afraid of death, the physical one, I mean. Then I saw the corpse of a woman I once knew. I was afraid to look at her, thinking that the image would circle around me for the rest of my life and make mine a living death. But someone forced me to look and when I saw the flesh decked out in funeral finery, that was all it was: flesh decked out in funeral finery. The real woman had gone. And my fears had gone. But why did I go to this funeral with my husband who didn't want me to anyway? Because… because… I don't know. But I did go.

The day was hot. My eyes were blinded by the sun. My throat was constricted. A friend had been hanged. They didn't even bother to blindfold him. I heard about it. They tried to hang him six times and each time something happened to stop them. On the seventh try they succeeded, though in their very success they failed. The man was dead but alive in me, just as much as my other friends. My dead friend, I heard, had made a quip about the tribunal that sentenced him to hang. He said that they reminded him of kangaroos. I had never felt the jump jump of kangaroos in my heart until the day of that burial. I remember reading nursery rhymes to my two-year-old daughter. I remember the scene very clearly. My daughter was sitting on my lap in the space under my protruding stomach and she was holding a large book of brightly-coloured pictures. I read to her about the three blind mice. See how they run. They all ran after the farmer's wife, who cut off their tails with a carving knife… My daughter screamed as we looked at the huge, ruddy-faced farmer's wife with a gleaming chopper in her hand and three tail-less mice who were wearing dark glasses – perhaps to show that they were blind. I tried to stop her from crying.

"Look, sweetheart, look! They're wearing sunglasses!" There were the three blind mice dressed up in waistcoats – and sunglasses. She stopped crying for a moment. Then she pointed to the severed tails of the mice, to the chopper and the ruddy face of the farmer's wife, and began to bawl again. I knew how she felt and tried to console her. At least the three blind mice were not dead... But then I looked at them again. They were as good as dead with their unseeing eyes, and with their tails cut off, they had no balancing sense. I called out to her nurse, a thin girl whom we had recently hired, beautiful in an androgynous way. She tiptoed into the room and whisked my daughter to her own room, a quiet place where mice did not wear sunglasses to hide their blindness and where the gleaming chopper could stay where it was: on the page.

Then it was that I heard about the hanging of my friend.

"So they murdered him?"

My husband shook his head slowly. "Don't let it upset you," he said. "They have decided that no one should make a martyr out of him. There's to be no public funeral," he whispered. "Even the churches... the pastors are not allowed to say anything."

I closed my eyes tight and pressed my hands on my stomach. The baby's movements reassured me. "Did you know that he predicted his own death?"

"You can't be serious."

"I'm very serious. He wrote me that he was going to die; that they would murder him and that they would hang him. He even wrote a poem about it."

My husband watched me guardedly, as if afraid to believe the truth of my words.

"If you doubt me, then go into the study – first drawer in the desk, to the right, the one where you keep your diary."

He disappeared and I began to muse on my bedside book, a Guyanese-published history of the Reverend John Smith and his missionary work in Demerara that I had brought with me from Guyana. How he, too, was the victim of injustice... Then my husband returned, his face ashen as he read the poem of my dear dead but alive friend. This is the poem:

THE HANGING

Victory
Is
The Lord's
They hanged me
on a day of bright sun showers ...

"Stop!" I shouted. "I don't want to hear any more. I'm going to the funeral."

"But it's... it's a secret and..."

"They wouldn't mind. I'm only a pregnant housewife," I managed to laugh shakily.

"And a writer, a writer," he said, his voice clipped. But he knew that when I was determined to do something, nothing would stop me.

So I went and saw the coffin, roughly hacked and put together with bright round tops of nails on the planks.

"Why Ikoyi cemetery of all places?" I asked my husband as we made our way through the tombstones. He didn't respond at first and when he did it was in an undertone – the breath of his whisper sounding loud in my mind.

"Actually, it's a bit of a masterstroke on the authorities' part. They believe that no one would guess that the body would be buried at so public a place."

"So this is a masterstroke?" The question hovered over the graves.

It was the graveyard of the well-to-do, the elite of the society. Angels in fashioned stone, wide-winged, watched as we stumbled over the weeds and gravel of serpentine trails coiled around and between the tombstones. Wreaths of flowers sat on some of the tombs and in the early morning they seemed a strange encumbrance, an uncalled for decorative disguise which could not fully protect the living from the knowledge of the dead.

The streets about were unusually silent, even though the

graveyard was in the vicinity of Obalende bus stop and the market. Overnight, sellers had thrown sacks over their produce and the numb mounds of onions, tomatoes and the tubers of yams looked all too like bodies. Vegetable bodies covered over, taken from earth.

"Why so many soldiers?"

"Don't ask so many questions, my dear. They are watching us."

Indeed they were. It is curious how a uniform negates and simultaneously asserts the wearer. There were five of them. They wore the green uniforms, berets and high boots with laces of the Nigerian army. The soldiers were in power. The guns shining at their waists and slung arrogantly over their shoulders, the laconic eyes which could be seen even behind the darkness of their sunglasses, said everything that was to be said about their position in the society.

Ikoyi cemetery is not that big, but it seemed big that day. It took forever to get to the spot where the soldiers stood, where the shallow grave was being dug in evident haste. One of the soldiers left his group and sauntered over to hurry us up. He shoved his gun into my husband's back.

"Walk fast, jare!" he shouted.

"My wife . . ."

"Why you bring woman with belly? Where your paper?"

"Oga soldier, I apologize. The, uh, man was a good friend of ours and…"

The soldier turned and, approaching the grave, urged the gravediggers to quicken their task. He extricated a kola nut from his pocket and began to chew rapidly, his eyes roaming beyond the graveyard, as if to ascertain whether Obalende was alive or not, whether there were many people about. Early morning workers were indeed beginning to trickle into the environs. The trestle tables and the heaps of vegetables were being uncovered in readiness for the day. The coffin – my eyes were drawn to it – lay by the side of the grave.

"Is enough! Grave done finish. This man be traitor to the federal republic of Nigeria," the munching kola-nut soldier declared. "Oh ya put coffin down."

The coffin was pushed into the grave. The planks had been hastily hammered together and one of them fell loose, exposing the wasted body of my hanged friend, his eyes still open, bold. The soldier spat at the face in a show of what he supposed was patriotic fervour.

"Traitor!" he screamed again. Then noting the obvious discomfiture of his fellow soldiers, their eyes riveted to their boots, he ordered the gravediggers to fill the grave with the earth that was piled beside it.

"Aren't you going to fix the plank?" I ventured.

"Oga, I beg, tell your wife to keep quiet, pata pata."

My husband put his arm around me and I discovered I was trembling. Some of the earth hit my face with a dank moistness. The gravediggers were flattening the earth on top of the grave with their spades, hardly pausing in movement.

"Oga soldier, could my husband please be allowed to say a very short prayer. He... he is a lay pastor."

The soldier was so astonished that he began to laugh. "You be oyinbo, no? Which country?"

I did not dare to reply.

"Tell your wife to keep quiet oh! I beg don't make me fit give report to my superior."

By this time I was past caring. They had hanged my friend on a trumped-up charge. They had held a kangaroo court in some crude semblance of justice. They had banned clergy, any church, from even mentioning his name.

"So, oga soldier, you have a superior! And who might that superior be? Could it be God by any chance?"

Before I knew it, the hard, leathery singe of a hand stung my mouth. I could taste salty blood. Really, feel it. My husband, without a word, put a dab of handkerchief to my mouth, a beseeching look in his eyes asking me to say nothing. Sweetheart, his eyes pleaded. Sweetheart, be quiet. These people are dangerous. Look what they have done to your friend. They believe they are in control of our lives and can do anything they choose. They believe they are gods.

"Get out, jare!" shouted the soldier and we left, walking slowly to the gates of the cemetery. There was me, my husband and the

18

brother and a cousin of my dead friend. With a shock I realized that our group had not said a word to each other throughout the burial – if you could call it that. It was a charade. A game to them, to El Presidente or Butcher Boy as we not so affectionately called him; he who thought he was the chief player of the game.

The car had been parked in a side road to avoid attracting attention, so we had to walk on the pavement and pass the market before reaching it. It took a long time to get out of the vicinity, for the petrol station by Obalende had opened at seven in the morning after having been closed for months. News spreads fast. Soon lines upon lines of vehicles were queuing, waiting for the petrol. Nigeria, a country which produces some of the best crude oil in the world, had now sunk to the level of importing petrol because... because...

"I did tell you. I did warn you against going to the funeral."

"Did I say anything? I'm glad I went; at least I did something."

"What you did," said my husband as he edged the car around a heap of debris, "was to antagonize... unnecessarily antagonize that soldier. Let's pray that your outburst doesn't reach the presidential mansion."

At home our daughter had turned on the radio and is delighted with herself. As I sit down – my husband in the kitchen warming some milk for me – the mechanical voice of the radio presenter pervades the room with a brisk insouciance. Obviously this particular newscaster is not the one who was hanged for openly condemning El Presidente. The President had come on TV some months back. Had announced that three hundred and sixty-five traitors to the nation had been shot on Bar Beach on his orders. And why? The President was fed up to his teeth with them. That's why. In the past year, he had grown tired of their mutterings about what they termed "political and economic slavery" and so he had three hundred and sixty-five traitors to the nation shot to represent every day of the year he had had to put up with them, their talk and their writings. Nigeria needed the military and in particular needed him. He was doing us a service. Salvation, the nation's freedom, came from him and him alone. Besides, had he not shown his alliance with God by keeping the churches open? God was on his side and on the side of the Federal Republic of

Nigeria. If God was not on his side then would he, the President, still be in power?

The newscaster is saying that Nigeria has been banned from the League of Nations for her anti-democratic crimes against humanity, for hanging poets. I wonder what this newcaster's fate will be?

John Smithers was sentenced to hang in Demerara in 1823. And ... and with an urgency of feverish spirit I knew that I would have to act quickly before the entire system of slavery, the seven characters in my head, did what they wanted to do. It was a case of the quick and the dead. I would do them in, pin them down on paper: John, Mary, Auntie Lou, the Governor, Quamina, Rosita, Captain McTurkeyen. The seven who wanted me dead.

But dead calm is what I am now and have to be.

I decide to call the novel *Three Blind Mice* because my daughter was so affected by that particular nursery rhyme. Apart from that, it seemed to me that both Demerara and Nigeria were in a state of blindness... Think I'll orchestrate things so that three characters, the females, will comment on the three men in their lives. And through their thoughts I shall give a kind of synopsis of the nursery rhyme and relate it to the happenings in Demerara.

I've only just returned from the funeral of my friend, so let me begin with another funeral. Here goes...

THREE BLIND MICE

They wanted my John hanged. They wanted to see him dead. They condemned him to death because they said he caused the slave revolt. That he was... What words did they use? "Instrumental in inciting the slave rebellion". And when they judged him and pointed at him in the dock, I saw the noose clear as daylight. It was a round noose of rope encircling the white neck of the colony and the black neck of slavery, all in a single circle. On that day, the day when the military tribunal gave judgment against John, I saw circles. Circles of nooses, and circles of necks and circles of eyes and the circle of my wedding ring around my finger. The circles, all of those circles, encircled me, Mary Smithers, wife of John Smithers, Reverend John Smithers. It seemed as if I was the only one who could see those circles.

For they were all blind. John Smithers, my husband; Quamina, the so-called leader of the slave revolt; and Governor Murrain, governor of the colony of Demerara. Three Blind Mice.

Did you ever see such a thing...? Father, forgive them. And forgive me for making John's life a hell on this earth. It could have been better. I, Mary Smithers, could have made it better. Now we're walking on and on in the dead of night. Me, Rosita and Auntie Lou. The three of us who wanted the freedom of a living life for all. But we had to struggle with our men who were blind. If only they had waited, if only they could have seen as I saw... things could have turned out ...

John, my husband, missionary-man; Quamina, the deacon of Bethel Chapel; and Governor Murrain. Three Blind Mice. See how they ran.

John to the grave of earth. Quamina to the yawning tomb of the sky, his head severed by the executioner's axe. Governor Murrain to the sea, dismissed from his post as governor, waving goodbye to Demerara, sailing to what he thought would be the sure horizons of England. Three Blind Mice.

John, if only you had listened to our eyes. To our vision. Where did it end? Walking behind this donkey cart with your coffin on this path? God. God. Good God.

Gingo is crouched in front, leading the donkey with a rope. A lantern is in his hand and he fumbles his way to the graveside. He is a thin man, stooping with the severe weight on him. The donkey, with its big drooping head, is blinkered, its neck pulled and strained by the rope harness as he pulls the rickety cart whose wheels lurch-grind over the little-used forest path. On the cart is a rectangular wooden box of planks hurriedly hammered together with bright nails. The tops of the nails are round silver discs which shine in the darkness. In the box is the body of Reverend John Smithers. The body is thrown to this side and to that, a thudding dead sound within the silence of a sky of deep covering black.

The trees are dense and mysterious, the palms whispering as they watch this man and the women, grieved with their inward thoughts: Gingo, the slave, leading the donkey pulling the cart on which lies the coffin in which tumbles John, the corpse; behind the woman-child, Rosita, whose head is bent – even in the dark this girl-woman is flower, is blossom, tenderness in her fingertips tracing the edge of the cart on which the coffin lies; beside her, Mary wonders at the sky's complacency; she sees the trees and thinks their acceptance of his death too silent when they should be crying, weeping and gnashing their rooty teeth, when they should be bringing down the limbs of their wooden selves with a bludgeoning force, crashing alongside them, before them on this footpath; and, at the rear, Auntie Lou struggles to keep up even with this, their slow-walking shuffle, muttering under her breath as they make their way to the grave.

They didn't want John to be a martyr – the military tribunal who sentenced death by hanging. Perhaps they did. Perhaps. They wanted to hear the gasping breath and see the vision of life escaping into gushing air. They were blinded in their own securities of flesh. The noose. A bit of cord around John's neck to squeeze the life out of him.

He wanted to suffer. He had a mission. He said it was God's mission. But I know it was his own. I know it. His mission was in his hair, bright orange. Red hair. Destructive. He wanted to die a martyr's death.

A blind mouse. See how he ran. Straight into the arms of the law which was not God's law. Which was God's law.

We trudge behind his coffin with a donkey half asleep guiding us through this forest of sounds. Contrived evidence. That's what it was. That he planned the slave rebellion with Quamina. That he refused to report it to the authorities. That he taught the slaves from parts of the Bible which he wasn't supposed to. All fabrication. Lies. They wouldn't listen to me. To us. We women. It was beyond their eyes to listen even if they had heard.

And that man who calls himself the Governor, with power of death in his governing hands, he killed my husband on the very day that they met at the celebration of his birth, as we danced in his honour in the governor's mansion. Sipped refreshing drinks which the slaves served, other slaves holding fronds of scented palm to prevent the mosquitoes from biting our exposed arms. The music was as genteel and unassuming as the laughter, the bantering and the chatter. The high ceiling had bright-coloured streamers and the long tables were covered with white linen cloth. On them sat dishes, bowls of the finest porcelain and the heaviest of silver cutlery; the crystal, heavy with its designs, winked at us with reflected mischief, which my dear husband could not see was in the making for him, and for us. For this entire colony of Demerara.

The Governor, Murrain, made his stance clear; his pronouncements were hard.

"Teach the slaves to read," he said, "teach them from parts of the Bible which let them feel all men are equal in the sight of God," he smiled, "and you teach them revolt."

John, my husband, reacted and pummelled them with his orange-haired words and his martyring intent, as blind as he was. As the mouse that he was. Blind mouse.

All their talk. For that's what it was. Lying, deceitful talk, even when I told them who was responsible for the slave revolt.

Governor Murrain does not have eyebrows, at least not so that you'd know. He has a cream-white forehead of never-ending flesh tinged with the pink flush of rum at his birthday party, and at the trial. There was no hope for my John.

Contrived evidence. Fabrication from the moment of the day at the dance when we all met. Lies.

Rosita is walking faster. Now she has caught up with Gingo. Their heads are bowed. Auntie Lou is bringing up the rear. Her breath is wheezing as she struggles along the path. Her bandana, a white coil wound around and around her head, seems to glow. Rosita turns, glances at me.

Rosita. John's love. He said… John said…

Rosita should not be here. They all ran after the farmer's wife. The three of them. John, Quamina, Governor Murrain. Why did they do it? Us wives. We wives. She was *only* a wife. A woman. An afterthought of crooked bone with a belated wish in it of companionship for the God-made man. She who nurtured seeds and souls. The farmer's wife. Did you ever see such a thing in your life? She led them on. They couldn't see the knife which sliced off their tales. They were blind. John, the missionary. John, the husband. Quamina, the Deacon of Bethel Chapel. Quamina, slave leader. Governor Murrain, the Governor of the colony. Governor Murrain, slave owner of men. Running, running, runnnnnnnnnnnnnnnnnnnnnnnn-nnnnning. Until the black gleaming knife of slave insurrection carved and sliced black and white.

Did you ever see such a thing…?

All this waste of black enslaved life and white life too. She cut off their tales with a carving knife right here in the plantations of Demerara. They cut off their own tails. Off-balance, they tumbled into graves of earth, air and water. Under my nose they cut my John into little pieces, with his spent body and his racking cough. He defied them. In a way. One blind mouse. To put him in a cell with no windows, the floorboards gaping to release the stench of water gone stale and putrid. All the talk and all the lies. To make him a scapegoat. Those whom he sought to save. Sentencing and condemning. I shall leave this place. As soon as we bury John, I shall leave. I shall never leave this place. This. This Demerara.

* * * * *

Mary had always resented her name. It was a blessing and a curse at the same time. It was the name of Christ's mother and it mocked her longing, motherless arms and heart. On good days, she would smile to herself and think Mary was ordained to sing magnificats. She wasn't. Not in this wretched hole of a place. Bringing up children here would be a reversal of that holy song. God knew what he was doing when he refused to bless them with offspring. And still the thought. And still the stillborn child. So still. So perfect. The little girl, a rose of sweetness. She did not live. Still the longing. Ring a ring of roses, a pocket full of posies. A tishoo, a tishoo, we all fall down. Falling in this harsh parchment of a colony.

She held the letter in her hands. Each time John loved her she would pray, her body stiff with hope. Each month the red betrayal, the biological violence against a dream. Each month her body was a psalm of tears. At school, the name Mary mocked her. The children had a rhyme… "Mary, Mary, quite contrary, how does your garden grow?" Her garden was sterile. In her womb nothing would grow. As sterile as the plantations which streamed their agony about her with hot, spiky, lonely knives of grass which refused to merge into the lush green oneness of her distant Hampshire. The plantations were alien and made her slightly afraid. There was no meeting point, only separate blades of grass. A wilderness which could only sprout black backs with gleaming cutlasses in the sun, bending and breaking. Over and over again. Over cane. Over sweet black bitter…

She was a slight woman, almost without breasts. Her hair was a whirl of chestnut, auburn. In moments of self-doubt, she would appraise herself in the mirror and brush it dementedly with Rapunzel hope, hoping for the knight in John to climb up and enter her, place his body over hers with love and release her with the chivalry of his Godly mission and his towering strength. Release her from this sterile emptiness, from the hot stone tower of this tropical life.

She smiled to herself. Still the dark medieval ages. Most times she would pull her hair back from her face. John loved her hair. But… Every day the Rapunzel in her accepted defeat. Until at night when the hairpins released her.

Her eyes were brown and flecked with gold, and her mouth, prettily curved, was a perfect rose. At least that was what he had said in their early months of marriage. There hadn't been much of a courtship. Just before the wedding they had met for tea after church. At that time John was living with Rev. Samuel Newley. The man thought very highly of John. In between mouthfuls of buttered scone, he looked directly at her glinting hair and addressed it benignly.

"John is a fine young man. No Christian woman could do better. A fine catch I'd say."

She had blushed and wished herself a million miles away. The wish had come true. One should be careful with wishes, even when your crooked little finger snaps a chicken bone in two. A sandwich between her teeth, she had felt the soft pale bread cleave to her gums. There hadn't been much of a courtship. Nothing to speak of really. He admired her hair and would sit for hours just gazing at it. His hair was more of an orangey colour, very bright. That was before they came to Demerara, this prison from which there seemed no escape.

She turned her mind to that fateful day when John received the letter. All the talk of Demerara; its jungles, rivers; that large freshwater fish called the arapaima – as big as a man. Things over there were larger than life. That fish... And those other fish, the piranha, which ate flesh. John had forced her to go into the interior of the country. To get the feel of the place. It seemed to be millions of miles away from Georgetown. There was no George there. No Englishness at all. Only the Amerindians with their thickened molasses hair weeping on their shoulders, the wide-swept land and the mountain, its tips roughly serrated, its body languishing down to meet patches of hot green spikes of grass – the Amerindians walking in a long, single file, dwarfed by the land, the mountain and the sky meeting it in a hot thin gauze of bandaged light. She could not see clearly and had to shade her eyes from the glare and feel the hot red blur of heat in her eyes. She had fainted. Her face was fanned; she had been given water from a flask. The blur had remained in her eyes and the fainting feeling had enveloped her so that she felt weak, like an insignificant ghost without a heaven to return to and without a God to guide her in the blurred reddened light, the sun and the silence. The immense silence of a continent and a land untamed by an English God.

It was their toes, their fingers which made her tremble – or rather their absence. Where a foot or a hand had dipped in water and the piranha, with their sharpened white teeth, had left them without the sibling communion of a five-fingered hand or a five-toed foot that could grasp the earth, or clasp a hand in friendship. Only their hair, the hair of the womenfolk, told the story: weeping in mourning black on bent shoulders. The continent was eating her whole.

She and John had been shown etchings on that day of the Demerara invitation. One of them was of Kaieteur Falls, the largest drop fall in the world. It looked like white hair whirling in frenzy. In spite of the nobility of the scene, it made her tremble. She had always been too sensitive. She had always felt more than she should...

Mary, Mary quite contrary...

How does your garden grow?

With silver bells and cockle shells

And pretty maids all in a row

That's how things should be. All in a row... The falls made her shiver. The Fall was what they were going for. To confront the elemental evil of the Fall. Water should run parallel. It should collect in streams and lakes and seas and rivers. It seemed like an aberration in nature that Kaieteur should stand erect and proud, as if in defiance of the law of gravity and God's own law.

She felt this. She felt all this. She took the envelope from him, and in that gesture she put her life into His hands and John's.

The following weeks were a flurry of activity. She packed medicines, quinine tablets, bandages. Their few clothes. Some books. She refused to part with her mirror. It was oval and rimmed with brass. She carefully wrapped it among sheets and blankets. She glanced at the envelope that spoke of another world and life. It was a sentence, a judgement.

* * * * *

"Mary, I'm worried about you. God knows I've got enough to do without your bother."

"Bother? My bother?"

"Ever since we've arrived in this colony you've been acting strangely. What's the matter? Is it the child?"

She toyed with her hair and murmured, "What child?"

"Our daughter. She's with God. It's the best way."

"And *she*, is she your child now?"

"What are you talking about, Mary? Rosita is... She must be eighteen years old or thereabouts..."

Mary laughed. A dry, hoarse sound. "We're all children of God aren't we, John? Rosita is responsible for the loss of my daughter."

27

"You lost the child before coming here. How can you possibly blame Rosita?"

"The Negroes can do things like that. I think it's called obeah. I think, my husband, Reverend John Smithers, that you had better be careful."

"Mary, my dear, you mustn't think of the child. She is with the angels."

"Have you noticed we've only started speaking in 'dears' since coming to this colony?"

"You should make yourself busy with..."

She spun around and faced him. "I have made myself busy, John. I have, I have. I look over your sermons. I sometimes teach the catechism class, although Quamina has been taking that of late... and I'm a founding member of the Salvation sewing and embroidery group for the female slaves ... and, and I love you."

She patted her hair. "I left everything to come with you, John."

He tried to smile but could not and noticed for the first time the fever in her eyes. Eyes which had once shone were now lost souls – wild. Mary began to cry.

"We're no good here. We're no good. The slaves don't learn anything. They're too tired. I don't blame them. We're not achieving anything."

John was suddenly angry. "I'm achieving. Rosita can now read her primer."

"She could read before we came here. Her English is perfect. Rosita, Rosita, ROSITA!"

A creamy-white girl entered the room.

"Madam, you called?"

She was absurdly beautiful. It was as if God had made her without the intervention of mere human beings. She was tall, very tall, and she had a habit of tip-toeing in a light bouncing movement, which was as graceful and as awkward as an eager schoolgirl's. She had long plaited hair which swung about her head.

Mary touched her own tresses. Rosita's hair was silky black. It had a tenderness in it, a streak of lightning too. But her eyes were her best feature. They were black as the dead of night and had an expression of deep sadness which belied her years. At eighteen she already had three children, a boy and two girls as lovely as herself. They were for one man, her common-law husband, Quamina. He lived on neighbouring plantation Success. He was allowed to visit her twice a week. Two days a week and three children. God was not fair. Anyway, the Negroes were more fertile. She had heard that somewhere.

Rosita was breathless. She had run in from the pantry where she had been washing fruit, and the water dripped from her bare hands and the clothes around her middle were wet so that the couple could see her navel, like a tiny bud mischievously peeking through.

John said, his voice low, "Rosita, would you prepare a meal of yams and stew for tonight?"

"Yes, do that, Rosita," Mary said, "and... and finish washing the fruit. I wouldn't want Auntie Lou to be distressed by your work. Do the washing, my dear, and try not to have a bath while you're doing it. There's a dear."

Rosita returned to the pantry and began to sing one of the new hymns she had learnt at chapel. Her voice floated beyond the couple who stared mutely at each other. There was no more to be said, but everything to be felt, everything to be understood.

* * * * *

Understood? The slim figure of the woman appeared strong as she moved back from companionship with Gingo to help Mary's shambling feet along the path.

Death was so complete. The night was a chattering lisp of insects. The palm trees stood erect like sentinels guarding them on their walk. It was a night of no moon. No rounded light with perhaps-a-man in it. Mary stifled a sob. It was not a crying out for the dead. It was a cry for what might have been between them. Her John. If only. She remembered their first argument about Rosita. Was it their first quarrel? Was it their last? And she had forgotten the content of John's sermon. She had left the house and then there was the corn that she had told Rosita to peel and then... that quarrel. But she wasn't really quarrelling about Rosita. The quarrel was with herself, her lacking self which sought and begged and yearned for his body and his soul – which he had given to the slaves.

A strangled scream erupted from her throat. Rosita made a signal for Gingo to stop the cart. The three froze. Auntie Lou was far behind. The donkey's ears flapped and its mouth turned down in a groan. The cart and the long rectangular box with the nails hammered on top of it was sharply etched in the night. A once upon a time John. And no, they did not live happily ever after.

O God... Oh John... My darling John. Maybe I was too possessive. I remember watching you as you slept. But that was before we came to Demerara. I'd look at you and feel greedy of the peace that slept under your face. Once I wanted to gnaw that peace away from you. But not just with my teeth. I wanted to suck it out of you so that I could be at one with you and God, so there would be no me-ness or you-ness left. No John-ness or Mary-ness. But I remember you laughing. You didn't laugh when I forgot about your first sermon.

Auntie Lou had joined them. She produced a handkerchief and wiped the sweat from her forehead. The party resumed their walk. Daylight was fast approaching and the dark whole of night gradually began to fade.

Perhaps it started then. I knew what your sermon would be about, and perhaps I didn't want to know... It was going to be on the "Peace that passeth all understanding"...and... I knew what you'd say. And then... Oh God, John... I forgot ... Your first sermon in Demerara and I forgot... I wanted to be too much to you, I suppose... and I suppose I just couldn't be. Now you have that peace that passeth all understanding.

She murmured "Understanding" and allowed Rosita to hold her. Gingo carefully put the lantern down. He blew on the wick. He motioned to Rosita to help him lift the coffin from the cart. The coffin was heavy even though John had lost so much weight during those last imprisoned weeks. The man and the woman pushed the coffin from the cart and it fell with a muffled thud. Some slaves had earlier been told to dig the grave and had been sworn to secrecy or pay the penalty of its disclosure with their lives.

They wanted him dead. Good and dead. Hanged by the neck. Unmartyred. The earth was fresh and moist and fecund.

"If I were a tree I would love to eat it," Mary muttered as she looked at the hole in the ground, making no attempt to assist the others with the coffin. They moved it as best they could and it fell on its side. Gingo cursed. Rosita, her face a study in serenity, edged herself into the grave and righted the coffin. Then she climbed out.

One of the planks had become unloosened and she stood peering at the wasted, dead face of the only man she, too, had ever loved. The digging was left to Gingo. He returned to the cart and picked up a spade and began to shovel the earth and dump it over the coffin. Some of the dirt hit Mary on the cheek. She put it in her mouth. She let the earth go round her mouth, licking, licking it with her tongue, around and around. And as if she couldn't have enough of it, she bent over, squatting by the grave, her hands tearing the earth in scoops, stuffing it into her mouth, forcing it down and licking the remaining particles around her lips. Licking, licking.

Gingo stood watching for a moment. Then continued with a frenzied digging like a man possessed, putting spadeful after spadeful of the earth into the grave. John's face under the exposed plank was not at peace. It was not at sorrow. It was just there.

"He might be sleeping. Maybe it's a mistake. Maybe he's not dead."

Mary scrambled towards the grave. Rosita attempted to restrain her.

"Madam Mary, please, please... master is dead. He is now in heaven. Be thankful."

Mary howled like a dog, an eerie sound which echoed and reverberated through the morning, now white and shrouded in a translucent film of mist. Gingo, his work completed, made the sign of the cross and replaced the spade in the donkey cart. The donkey had been quietly dozing until he heard the sound of Mary's howling. Ears outstretched, all a quiver, he snorted once and began a grotesque hee-hawing. Mary struck Rosita on the face.

"If it hadn't been for you, he might still be alive. You're all liars. The Governor is a liar. Those slaves – Paris, Bristol, Aggie – who swore on oath that John planned the insurrection... All liars."

And lie upon her. And lie with her. John the liar. That quarrel came upon her again. When was it? Five, six years ago?

And she heard herself speak as if from a distance.

John, I must know. Are you giving that slave lessons in reading and writing alone?

What slave?

Rosita... You know who I mean. Rosita.

Oh. Rosita. Sometimes I teach her the catechism...Why?

Do you sleep with her, John?

Each night I am at your side sleeping. Each morning I awake at your side.

Do you make love to her, John? Were the vows you made to love me, honour and cherish me as your wife. . . the vows you made to God deceiving? My God, how you've changed in this climate.

People change. It is in the nature of things to change. I think some intellectual must have said that at some time… It is in the nature of…

John… Do you, have you ever made love to her?

Yes, once. In a way. Only once. And then it was…

You're lying. You must be lying. I'll get your evening drink… It's so hot. We should never have come to this godforsaken place… It is so very hot.

Mary sighed. She seemed as spent as the man in the coffin. As dead. The group walked the miles back to the plantation.

Except for Auntie Lou. She remained by the graveside, her arms folded.

★ ★ ★ ★ ★

My arms will never fold until this novel is completed. The memory of graveside walking. The execution of my friend, a death by hanging, is still with me, close-hanging me.

I feel faint as my young daughter touches my stomach and asks me if I want water. A glass of water. Perhaps a simple thing like a drink of water will quench this thirst bellowing inside me where my unborn baby sleeps.

My husband is concerned. "I told you, my dear, not to attend the burial; not in your condition."

I am angry with the commonplace drear of "my dear" and I sulk.

"I have to write this novel. Mary and Auntie Lou and Rosita have just finished burying John."

"Don't get too caught up in the novel. You must learn to relax."

He is so kind I could explode with anger and kill the child I hold within me. I must learn to be in control.

"What if I have a miscarriage?"

"Don't think of such things. Leave everything to God."

"It's all very well for you, isn't it?"

A certain silence.

"Isn't it?" I shriek at his impassive eyes.

My toddler asks me to read a nursery rhyme and she shows me a picture of Contrary Mary kneeling in a garden of flowers. The words stick in my throat as a sudden wrenching pain stabs me. My baby is dying.

He reaches for the telephone. "I told you not to go to the funeral." His hands are shaking.

"They hanged my friend."

The ambulance will be on its way soon. I cannot speak. The pain is excruciating.

"Where's the nurse?"

This nurse is always there whenever she is needed; that alone makes me mad.

"I'm feeling better," I say, even though I'm feeling worse. Much, much worse.

Nurse is packing some of my nightdresses and underwear in an overnight bag. There is a smile on her lips and she is humming a tune. A hymn. I don't know the words of this hymn. I pull in my breath and tell her to bring me lots of paper and a pen; she is to put them at the very top of my overnight case. She gets my writing notebook and not the loose sheets of paper which I requested, but I am too much involved with this wracking, churning pain and I feel an ooze of hot trickling down the sides of my thighs. My husband is downstairs waiting for the ambulance to arrive.

"Bring me a piece of paper!" I am screaming at her lovely braided black hair.

Nurse brings me the sheet of paper and a pen and I make her sit down as I draw a long pole with a bar shooting away from it in a reversed seven. I draw a square at the bottom of the pole. Nurse has a vague smile on her lips. I am having a miscarriage and she is having a vague smile on her lips. The pain subsides.

"Madam, should I get you some napkins?... Your dress. . ."

There is blood on my dress; it is dark red and it spreads in the shape of a fantastic flower; larger than life is this flower with petals of blood.

"Do you see this sheet of paper?"

She nods her head. She is not blind.

"I am going to play a game with you. It's called the Hangman's Game."

I look at her pretty-pretty face to see the effect of my words.

"It sounds rather gruesome, Madam."

She is my nurse and she has such a wide-ranging vocabulary! Nurse is only eighteen. For years I had been doing all of my own housework and managing it very well, thank you. Then this pregnancy came along and the doctors said I should take things easy if I wanted to keep my unborn child. Nurse, I refuse to name her, was my husband's suggestion for a house-help. He said I needed someone to assist me with the cooking, the cleaning of the house and taking care of our little daughter. Then Nurse, this beautiful girl of eighteen, joined our household. She had done well in her secondary school examinations, but had not the necessary funds to continue with her university education. In the meantime I decided I would educate her. She is the main culprit in this Nigerian/Demerara drama for now, I think. I will hang her first.

I draw seven dashes below the hangman's edifice like this:

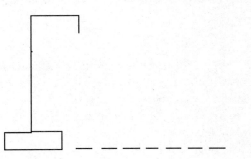

Her eyes open wide. "Madam! I…"

"Shhhh… it's only a game. Besides it will help take my mind off the pain."

"Madam, you will not lose your baby – in the name of Jesus."

Nurse is a Christian. So am I. So is my husband. We are all, all Christians. Not the Sunday-only-Church- going-type of Christian you understand. We try to live the teachings of Christ daily. It's not easy. As a matter of fact, you could say Nurse came into my household in response to our faith, complete with a tiny gold cross hanging around her neck. She had been introduced to us by her mother, a deaconess in the church whom everyone calls "Mother of Nurse", because the nurse looked like a nurse even when she was younger. The deal was that in exchange for helping me with the housework, we'd pay for her university education. I planned to give her an education she would never forget.

"This is how the game is played," I say. "Listen carefully. Each blank represents a letter in the alphabet and the letters together make a word."

"What word?"

"I'm the one who knows the word."

In spite of my pain, I somehow felt strong.

"I think I've heard of this game, Madam, but…"

"It's my game!" I shriek, noting her pouting lips which are curved ever so prettily. I repeat the words softly. "It's my game. You have to guess the first letter."

"But Madam!" she protests. "There are twenty-six letters in the alphabet!"

"Precisely so, and if you don't get the word soon you'll have to go!"

"Madam?"

"You heard me."

My husband appears. I had been so intent on teaching Nurse the game that I hadn't heard the sound of the ambulance arriving.

"My dear, you need to change your dress."

Nurse goes to my wardrobe and selects a huge maternity dress and shoves it over the one I was already wearing.

"You have three guesses in the first instance."

I smile slowly at the vacancy in her eyes.

"H, Madam."

"No, it isn't H," I say. "There are no Hs in the word I'm thinking about."

"P, then, the letter P."

"No Ps either." I am feeling deliriously happy and the P, which made me think of pain, my own pain, becomes a gentle stabbing throb. I feel weak but force myself to stand.

"What on earth are you two playing at?" demands my husband, staring at my drawing of the Hangman's Game. "Sweetie, what is the meaning of this? I knew something like this would happen. I did warn you not to attend the funeral!"

"Well, it's a bit late for that isn't it, sweetie?" I retort.

Nurse and my husband exchange glances. She seems to gain a certain confidence.

"Shouldn't you give me a clue, Madam?"

So she wants a clue. Fair is fair. And fair can also be foul, as King Macbeth learnt to his cost. Who cares? I'm not going to play the Hangman's Game with Nurse in the usual way – which is to throw a dice for a number six to determine whose turn it is to give clues, letters etc. I'll think up each clue and call all the shots. Bam! Bam! Like that. This game will be played without dice.

"So you want a clue for the first letter?"

I direct my words to my husband and give what in books they call a wry smile. "This Nurse wants a clue. She's been reading my book, I think."

"What book?"

"The book I'm writing, of course… on the last slave insurrection which took place in Demerara."

"Why don't you concentrate your energies on the present, on reality, on Nigeria?"

"Why on earth should I? I want to escape what's happening here."

He shakes his head. "Sweetie, do get a move on. Your situation could be serious."

"Oh it's very serious. More serious than you could ever imagine."

I can see he is losing patience.

"Well imagine this, sweetie. You are my wife. You're having a miscarriage and if you don't get a move on we won't be imagining the loss of our child."

"What child?"

"The child you're carrying."

He comes towards me and slowly walks me through the room, across the floor and down the stairs to the front door where the ambulance, along with two uniformed attendants, stands waiting. The men sit me down not so comfortably in the ambulance and my husband blows me a kiss as the doors are shut.

"Aren't you coming with me to the hospital?"

"Have you forgotten it's fellowship day? Nurse can go with you. I'll be of more use to you, to us, if I'm praying for you and the baby."

My head begins to reel. "Nurse cannot come with me – who will look after our daughter while, while…?"

I can feel myself fainting, going under, and it is not an unpleasant feeling.

As the ambulance gathers speed on its way to the hospital there

37

is a sudden jolt and my head feels clear again. "Driver! I want to go back."

"But Madam!"

"I must go back!"

The man reluctantly reverses the vehicle and when we reach the house, surprisingly enough, I see my husband and Nurse standing by the open door. Nurse holds my daughter by the hand and, looking closely, I see dirty smears of soil around my daughter's mouth. She must have slipped out of the house to pick flowers in the garden and used this opportunity to eat some earth.

"Thank heavens you've come; that's my sweetie! Here's the overnight bag. Wonderful that you remembered it the state you're in."

"That's not why I came back! Nurse, this is the clue for the first letter in the Hangman's Game – the fact that you're a nurse."

As if listening to a voice outside myself, I hear dry cackling laughter coming from my throat. Nurse stares at me blankly.

"Well, what's the letter?"

"Madam, we really must be going." This the driver of the ambulance. His eyes are anxious.

My husband shrugs his shoulders wearily. "Answer her, tell her the letter for goodness sakes, whatever it is; humour her."

Nurse touches one of her long black braids. They were so long she could have tied them around her throat and still have some braids hanging under her flower of an eighteen-year-old face. Her hair has possibilities.

"Madam, it is the letter K for kindergarten."

"Wrong again! You're wrong. Bye! Let's go to the hospital."

Through the ambulance window I look at the two figures vanishing into the distance. So she knows. Nurse knows that nurses work in kindergartens. The girl is too educated for her own good. After they've checked up on me at the hospital, I'll fill in the first blank on the paper on which I'd drawn the gallows. The dead man's round circle of head will be on the paper. Not only did they want me dead, they wanted to take my unborn child away from me too. It isn't going to happen. Not with my own words.

I know *that* even before the doctor says, "You've been lucky.

You should stay and rest in the hospital for a few days."

"I'm to be pampered, am I?"

"Most assuredly."

"Can I at least continue with the writing of my novel?"

The doctor seems surprised at my urgency. "If you promise you won't overdo it."

"Most of it is in my head."

"Of course it is, my dear."

I ask his departing back to send a hospital nurse to my room. When she comes I'm glad she's wearing a white uniform and not the ankara wrappers that my own nurse usually wears. She unzips my bag and brings me the sheets of paper which I'd placed on top of my things. On the first blank, I write a triumphant curve of the letter C. C is for CHILD. Mary's child had been stillborn. My child is alive. I, a Mary or not, would sing magnificats. I had hanged intent. I had won the first round in the Hangman's Game. Let me write and see what they think they've got in store for me….

★ ★ ★ ★ ★

As they left John's grave, Mary thought the walk would never end. The donkey, Gingo made their way to the house...

Do I regret this taking of life of men who refused to see? I tried with John but he was innocent and blind... He saw the Words but not the light. Why did he have to be so very blind? I did try. I did try to make him see with his heart. John, oh my dear John. God, will you not come down in a fleshy miracle? Why did John not love me? Why wouldn't he take me seriously? Why didn't he believe in me? Why this madness?

★ ★ ★ ★ ★

So they plan to make me mad. I should have guessed it. First by depressing me with thoughts of a child who will die stillborn. That has not happened. That will never happen. There are six more letters to fill in. I already have the C. My unborn child is safe. But I must hurry. Only God knows what they are plotting for me. They do not know that I am the one with eyes that can see. They, my male characters especially, are blind. They live in the nineteenth century. They cannot wear sunglasses. I don't think sunglasses had been invented at that time.

It is pleasant to be in this hospital room, lying here on this bed. There is a faint smell of antiseptics and medicines that cure, and the light which flows through the window is a vague tremor of the long line of the sun. I must get back to the novel. I hope Rosita will be good. I hope she will live up to the sweet flower of her name in her dealings with Mary. If not... even now she has not dealt well with Mary. Treasonous thorns from the stem of the rose scratch her thoughts as she walks back from the grave to the plantation.

★ ★ ★ ★ ★

Rosita could not help comparing the two men, John and Quamina. When Quamina said her name it brought out the thorns. But John had touched the softness in her name. They had only loved once… if you could call it that. But that once was enough to take with her through the lifetime of his death. She hadn't wanted to attend the first sermon, shunned the confrontation, the hurting knowledge of her want. She had longed to delay its inevitability one day more, one day at the very least. So, beside the wall of the chapel, she'd sat on the grass listening, a basket of corn between her outstretched legs. She tore the outer leaves of the corn while listening to his voice, his voice preaching to the slaves and to Quamina her husband, only stopping to cough, to tell them about God, the father, the son, and the peace that passeth all understanding. She stroked the silken hair of the corn. She rubbed the corn on her bare arms. Her eyes closed.

A buckra passed, glanced with a quizzical, amused air. She saw the handlebar whiskers of McTurkeyen, the way the spurs cut deep into the horse's flesh. She hastily gathered the corn into the basket, left it by the chapel wall and went in.

Their eyes met. He beckoned her to come closer, and she sat, her head bowed. Longing to look up and feel his eyes. Knowing that he knew.

She sees John looking down from the pulpit at scrubbed benches dotted with so many slaves; and John slaving too, so pale against the heavy heat, preaching promises of life to come and the meaning of His Word.

She had to pull it out of him, see him fall in flesh, feel certainty; that the spirit loved before it flagged, like a wilted lily gone false-eastering.

The service over. The slaves with their complaints. The long walks from Bethel Chapel to distant plantations: Rachel, the elder midwife in the area, trying to cling to other lives not physical, her hands grasping a Bible which she could not read, a Bible torn and eaten by rats – she wanted a new one; Quamina, officious as ever, urging the others to get back to their plantations. They had to avoid the whip. John, his retching cough. His body listening.

She dragged her feet outside, wanting to be the last.

"Why didn't you come earlier?"

She pointed to the basket of corn. "The corn could not wait."

She ran as fast as her legs could carry her to the main house. She looked over her shoulder and saw him leaning against the wall of the chapel. He seemed burdened and weary. The sins of the world humped on his slender back, in the cough which racked him. He couldn't deny the weight on his back.

★ ★ ★ ★ ★

"You're working very hard, Ma'm." The hospital nurse is cheery. I am tight-lipped. She pushes one of those tables with wheels over to my bed so that I am forced to drop my papers on the floor. I will do anything she says… All I want is to be left alone in peace to write the next bit of my novel in which Rosita accompanies Mary back to the manse after the burial. Auntie Lou is left alone by the graveside, her arms folded. Rosita, woman-child that she is, is thinking about her dead master and how she loved him. The little wretch.

"You don't seem to be in a good mood, M'am," says the nurse with concern. "You should be happy that your baby is fine. A few months more and you'll be holding him in your arms."

"I will have a daughter, another daughter."

"Of course you will, Ma'm. A daughter it shall be." She moves closer to me and pushes me forward so that she can prop up the pillows. I feel very comfortable. The naked white austerity of the room, its antiseptic atmosphere, is cleansing. All of a sudden I am very hungry at the sight of the covered dishes the nurse places on the table and the tasty aroma of something I cannot discern. It is a smell of food that belongs to my childhood and the nursery. She uncovers the dish and I see a mass of white. It is corn meal porridge.

"Would you like some milk and sugar with it?" The nurse smiles solicitously. "I've got a special surprise for you," and she uncovers the sugar bowl to reveal a dark gold mound of glittering crystals. "Demerara sugar," she crows. She is using that tone of voice which grownups usually adopt when speaking to children. It's a namby-pamby voice and I hate it.

"Leave me alone, please."

I can see that she is upset that I am not showing any pleasure at this particular surprise. She departs and, bending over, I put the dish of porridge on the floor and exchange it for the pile of papers: my novel.

Rosita is in a mind-set. As set as the congealing porridge. She dares to think of John Smithers as hers, does she?

★ ★ ★ ★ ★

The next morning found Rosita making corn porridge for the Smithers, the pap smooth and pale. John came up behind her, his voice startling her.

"Why are you in the kitchen at this hour?"

"I usually rise at five in the morning. Besides, Madam is leaving early today. She is going to Bachelor's Adventure plantation with two other madams. Many slaves are sick there."

"They are indeed," said Mary entering the room. She sat at the table spooning the porridge.

"Rosita, this food is for babies. Don't make it again. I don't like corn prepared in this way. Although God knows, by the time I've finished with those sick slaves, I'll need all my strength."

"Do stop complaining, Mary..." John began.

He stood by the doorway. He always seemed to be standing at entrances. He never remained in any enclosure for long. Perhaps he felt more comfortable this way. He needed the support of a door.

"She peeled the corn, lots of it. You might at least try to eat some porridge..."

In answer Mary got up to leave as she heard the sound of a carriage draw up outside the house. Mrs. Pearsons and Mrs. Gruegel had been prompt as usual. She kissed John on both cheeks, donned her bonnet and went to meet her friends. Soon John and Rosita could hear the clatter of horse's hooves, the grind of wheels as the carriage left the plantation.

John was still standing by the door. "I like corn," he announced. And then with the beginnings of a smile, "I love corn." She did not look up. He noticed her nervous hands and, as if with a sense of resolution, he gathered his jacket in his arms like an almost forgotten child and strode hurriedly out of the house. He was on his way to the chapel.

The steel gates of the chapel were locked. He tried to open them. He shook them angrily with a strange despair. Foreboding. The sky darkened above him and he turned to go. Perhaps it would rain, rain in torrents and blot out everything from his worldly existence. Perhaps an ark would appear. Demerara in flood, and the ark to protect God's children. Protect him from certain sin. He could not prevent it. Rosita. It was a sin to harbour fleshly thoughts. He began to cough so hard that his entire being coughed with him. He felt tired and devoid of strength. It might rain. God would send him a sign. Any sign. An ark. A lumbering great boat like a house in this sea of slavery. Why did God allow this service of the flesh? Why did he not provide an ark when he, John, was about to commit the sin of his adult life? Why, when he needed it most, did God not come down and point his finger to show the way? God must have built the ark in regions such as these. Untamed hells. Far from the domesticated hell of England, which could contain and shoulder guilt from afar.

Rain in England was tea-time rain. There, one could look out of the windows and see pearly drops in a benevolent pitter-patter making the grass green and lush. Rain in Demerara was torrential, with the avenging force of Old Testament fury to lash and whip mortals. Rain here was floods without ark promises. Rain in England was New Testament – with growth in water and baptismal fonts. Heaven sent. Perhaps it would rain English rain. If it rained, he would not... He would not feel the flesh. Rosita.

It did not rain. Surely she could not be a sin? Oh God please help me. Please do not let me. It did not rain. He walked to the house, trying not to run. Running to sin. She was there, her eyes waiting, and she held out her hand. He felt its cold clamminess and grasped it tightly. He was pulling her up the stairs. The furniture, the dining room table, the chairs, the clock on the mantle piece gazed, impassive. The window, the curtain drawn back, was a huge eye.

"Not here... not here," she whispered. "I know a place. I shall go with a basket. You follow. We shall have to... in case..."

"How did you know?"

"I saw it in your eyes... in the chapel... and then the corn."

Their laughter. A trickle of water.

An elderly tree overshadowed them, its branches drooping with dark heavy leaves so that their faces were patterned.

She saw that his eyes and hair were bright and when she touched him and he sought her mouth, her eyes burned.

47

"Nothing happened."

"Nothing happened."

"I so wanted to touch. My dear sweet Rosita, this must never happen again. I, I, am a man of the cloth... I am a married... I cannot... I..."

She touched his ear lobe.

"Never again."

* * * * *

Even in their love, longed-for, urgent, and unconsummated, John had remained concerned for her. The slaves. Quamina.

In the early hours of the morning, the wee hours, the palm trees were supple-bending adolescent girls, their night-hardness gone. They swayed in the gentle breeze, in a huddle, in a whispering, secretive, huddle, their heads bending, and in their limbs a waiting-touching-secrecy.

That was how it had been with them. A joyous secret. Like the first four months of pregnancy when only the mother knows and harbours the secret of a life within. She'd had three children for Quamina, and nothing of those three burdens of love and pain was the burden of love and pain she felt for John. She would carry its weight to the grave. His confined soul would distend, extend her very self. She had to be strong. John was dead. Quamina – another man, the same mission – he, too, was dead. He had been a good husband. Unlike so many, he did not sleep with other women. His real woman was the desire for freedom. He wooed her. He fought for her, for the freedom of the slaves. He was free now. As free as a bird. As free as the vultures that circled round and round the stump of his head with its once rolling eyes on the spiked gate of Plantation Le Resouvenir, implanted for everyone to see – those who sought to be free men.

He had been a short man, but in death he was tall. He resembled the Ashanti stools of his tribe with the dignity and royal blood flowing in the bandy legs with toes splayed out. His skin was black and dull and eye-soothing; his eyes round, the whites hard and glassy-oiled like the fried white of eggs; his speech guttural and unpleasant to her ear. He had a habit of suddenly raising his arm to his brow and sweeping the collected sweat onto the floor or field. She had always been intrigued by that. It seemed a fertilizing act, as if the salty water would pour in torrents around him and stimulate growth – and he did have the gardener's gift. In the portion of land assigned to him, onions, tomatoes, yams and corn grew so thickly and provided so much surplus that they always had enough to sell on market days. Together, in the early years of their marriage, they had fished at night to supplement the saltfish ration given to the slaves. Added to the enormous amount of food that Auntie Lou stole from the Governor's kitchens, they and their children were probably the best fed slaves on the plantation.

In the beginning, Quamina had always played with them, spared the time to take the chigoes out of their feet and tell them a story, or take them fishing, even when the cane had to be brought in and the work was heavy. Then came his mission. The plan was to get as far as the East Coast, live in the bush along with other slaves from Georgetown and return and seize the freedom which he was sure was coming. It went wrong from the very beginning.

Auntie Lou had had a dream on the eve of his departure. She could not fathom the meaning of the dream but it was clear that Quamina would not survive. Auntie Lou had dreamt of mice and they were blind. They scrambled into her hut and she woke with the noise. She picked up a broom and tried to hit them; the more she hit them, the more they squealed and ran bouncing into the door, the table, the bed, the chair. Their tails were long, livid cords and in their black, enraged blindness they formed a circle in the middle of the hut and their tails, as if possessed of a life of their own, knotted together in coiling agreement. Auntie Lou picked up a chopper, and descended on them. The chopper hit a tail. But still the circle of mice remained. The only sound was no sound. Auntie Lou woke up.

When Quamina was not attending chapel on the days he could get a pass, Rosita would watch him lying on her bed, arms crossed over his chest. Sometimes he spoke aloud, as much to her as to himself. It was a guttural monotone that seemed to go on and on, almost as if he was praying or steeling himself for some purpose. She tried to tend the wounds of his soul and help him.

Auntie Lou had said a revolt would have to have superior weaponry, superior to that of the buckras. They had to be organized. Any rebellion would have to be organized. Quamina had failed in his first attempt at revolt. His back was whipped to shreds and his fingers squeezed with iron clamps until the bones broke and his fingers left misshapen. She, Rosita, had mended the broken fingers and restored a new gift to his gardening hands, but the only balm that would cure his soul was freedom. He was determined to be a free man and determined that his lost children – their lost children – sold in his sight by McTurkeyen, the punishment for running away, would be free. It was the only energy left in him. He became Deacon of Bethel Chapel, a model Christian. He made it his business to attend the sick beds of those with smallpox in the company of Auntie Lou. Many a night, with or without a pass, he sat with Auntie Lou talking and talking. He and the men would gather in her cabin. Sometimes he would interpret in his own Quamina way, sections of the Bible John Smithers preached from. It was the only time a smile puckered his lips.

★ ★ ★ ★ ★

50

Why can't the people in this hospital leave me in peace? It's the nurse again.

She asks me, "Ma'm, where's the porridge?"

I point to the floor.

"But you haven't touched it. You have to keep your strength up, you know."

Behind her is my husband and Nurse. My husband is standing at the entrance of the room, leaning on the door frame. The way he leans on the door is irritating. I can hardly see his face because he has a huge bouquet of flowers that hides it. Nurse, unbidden by me, sits on one of the hospital chairs. I don't think I am happy, but I want to be. It is raining outside, a drizzle of dicing lines which fall and pierce the green-grassed ground of my heart.

"I thought you'd be glad to see me," murmurs my husband, placing the bouquet of flowers on the bedside table. He motions to Nurse and she puts the flowers in a vase of water.

"I've got a surprise for you," says my husband.

Not another one, I think. I have had enough surprises for one day and even for a lifetime. I do not need surprises. I need control. He has the control. Perhaps it comes from him giving his life to Christ. For it is written; yes, it is written. If you give your life to God... if you submit to God, then curiously enough you are free. I want to taste that freedom. I want to gorge on it. Nurse smiles at me. She has those long black braids of hers wound around her head. I'm staring at the long ropes of them and thinking hanging thoughts. I put a protective hand on the round of my stomach.

"How are you feeling, Madam?" comes her caring question.

She looks so innocent, as if butter wouldn't melt in her mouth.

"I, I, was the one who sent you the special Demerara sugar."

It would be her, wouldn't it? She would be the one to send me sweetness for my tea and not know about the slave deaths that the

51

cane crop caused. She has been reading her geography book. She knows I am a native of Demerara. She also knows why I came to Nigeria in the first place. In an unguarded moment I told her that I wanted to write a book on slavery, to delve into the reasons why slavery happened. I had already been to England on a grant, ironically given to me by the British Council, to research the European point of view. It seemed logical to visit Nigeria, Africa, after that. I had married. I had stayed.

I am determined not to utter a single word. My husband puts his hand on Nurse's shoulder. The hand of my husband brushes a petal from the shoulder of Nurse and my eyes hurt with sunhurt at this brushing of a petal. I have only been away from home for a few hours and today, from my reclining view, I see this brushing.

They both watch me. Nurse turns to face my husband. He turns his face away from hers.

He says to me, "You forgot to bring your Bible." And then inconsequentially, "Our daughter is very well."

Of course our daughter is well. C is for child. C is for confidence.

I begin to write words beginning with C. Positive words.

"I know the word, Madam!"

"What word?" I forget myself and speak. I can see that they are relieved.

"The C word! It's culpable."

Not so bright are you, little girl woman of a nurse...?

"The word has seven letters."

My husband frowns. I smile. I am almost happy until the door is pushed open. This person doesn't even knock. My eyes first see a bandy pair of legs and then travel up to the head of a stunt of a man. His shortness has a beautiful brevity of inner propulsion as he comes into the room. Apparently he is expected by these two, the husband and Nurse. She jumps up, nearly knocking over the vase of flowers on my bedside table.

"Who is he?" I ask.

My husband interjects. "This is your new steward. He also happens to be Nurse's cousin and betrothed."

"Betrothed? You're engaged to your cousin?"

The man stands to attention like a soldier. "I hope you won't mind me helping round the house." His accent is guttural. "I can be your gardener. I can. . ."

I close my eyes. So this is Quamina. He is now our gardener and general dogsbody.

The hospital nurse bustles in. "I think Madam should get some rest..." her speech tails off. Nurse grates her chair on the floor and I open my eyes.

"The clue to the next letter is blind." I say these words quietly.

"Blind?" she repeats.

"Blind." I affirm.

She opens her mouth to speak.

I say, "I'll be more explicit, Nurse. The second letter of the word relates to this clue... People didn't know that the best-selling author of the world had written Him into the script of our lives. They were blind."

"I suppose, Madam, that you are referring to Jesus? The prophets foretold... I think that the letter must be 'o' for obscure."

She's right – in a way – but I cannot let her win a single letter of the game, and I tell her, "From the sound of your voice I can tell that your O is a small O. And what's more, I wasn't thinking of 'obscure' but 'obscurantize'."

"I haven't heard of that word before, Madam."

"Now you have."

My husband kisses me on the cheek and promises to bring me my Bible on his next visit and I think they want me to fold my arms in sleep like Auntie Lou at the graveside, thinking her thoughts about John and of the deaths and the revolt. They want to obscurantize me. Yes, that's it. At least I've got this child in me alive and kicking. Nurse will never get the word in the Hangman's Game. She is as blind as my male characters who seek blind control over self and over other selves. So I'll write about Auntie Lou as she sits at the graveside of John Smithers.

They are staring at me.

"As you can see," I tell them, "I'm anxious to continue writing. And Nurse, have you ever thought of cutting your hair?"

"What are you going on about?" asks my husband. "Perhaps we should leave. You obviously need some rest."

"I'm fully rested, thank you."

"I think we'd better go," says my husband again, pecking me on the cheek. I grab him by the shoulders and give him a full kiss on the mouth. He is embarrassed.

Nurse dutifully looks out of the hospital window. The betrothed of Nurse crosses over to the bed and gives me a handshake with a limp hand; it is wet with moistness and I cannot prevent myself from immediately wiping my own hand on the bedsheet. Nurse and her fiancé quit the room. My husband remains.

"You're sure you're alright?" he smiles. I feel sorry for him and I pull him over and hug him and tell him I'm fine.

★ ★ ★ ★ ★

Auntie Lou made herself comfortable. She always felt at peace in the presence of death. There was something soothing about the repose of the dead, even when the death was untimely like John's. Sitting there on a log she let her thoughts ramble.

All o' them is the same. All o' them. Take here the Reverend Massa Smithers. He come here to this colony and he want preach to we. He want make we learn 'bout top and bottom and God. But he in realize what he up against. He talk talk and he in see. Is only mouth he got. If you going teach slaves – "Servants be obedient to them that are your masters" – in one breath, then on the other hand teach them 'bout Jesus Christ and sinners and Jesus coming down to save all o' we. . . Is what you going expect? He better dead. The man so stupid he in know what goin' on. Is Mary and Rosita and me who plan this thing what they does call revolt. Is we who do it. And no one will thank us for it. Cause is a world of men. All o' them blind.

Look at Quamina. He the worse of the lot. I shoulda warn Rosita 'bout he. He use the chapel; he use John to plan the thing in he no see way. Every time he come over to see Rosita he don't got time for she. He only thinking 'bout freedom. Well he got it now. They chop off he head and put it on a spike. He in even take time. Is just, "We gotta have we freedom. We gotta and King George say so." Where is King George? Sitting on he ass in England talking 'bout pardon and things gotta change. He ever been out here? He ever come to Demerara? He ever see we down here? All of them buckra them talk talking 'bout emancipation in fine building in parliament and thing and they in know a damn 'bout how we does suffer. And it not only the revolt. Is all the time they does make us small 'cause we black. They lash we with cat-o-nine on all-we bare back; they put we in the stocks; they don't want we with we pickney 'cause they does sell mother, husband, baby, child on the block. And they enjoy it. They not going to give up *that* fast.

Quamina too stupid foolish. All a could have tell him, all a could have say... If you want freedom you must have to wait for the correct time. You have to wait for when the women go tell you is time. Cause time and woman always agree. You have to know 'bout time if you is a woman. Is not only when you monthly time does come with blood, is also the time when you going to birth pickney. Man don't know 'bout time. They all too true blind. All of them. Quamina, I did say if you want freedom, wait. It going come. The women them going get the freedom for you. All a could have tell him, all a could have say... We gotta plan good good. And we did plan good. But no... he can't listen. He blind like the rest o' them. Can't see nothing. He make the men on all the plantations hungry and big-eye for what they could take. Oh God... when Govna get those bucks and that big fart McTurkeyen to hunt him down, I coulda dead. He give them musket and too much shot. As if the bows and arrows not enough. I wonder when they goin' take off he head from the gate... the place smelling bad bad and the flies... Well, when you can't see pass you nose, what you can expect?

She was tired and the trees, the bushes, listening as they were, made her want to remain where she was. She glanced at the big black Bible, which Mary in her anguish had left behind. There it was, on the ground. She picked it up; making a fist, she thumped it. She threw it down; she kicked it out of the way.

All o' them blind. Especially Govna. That man. That man needle me. All three o' them needle me. But Massa Govna needle me the most. I shoulda stick a pin in he ass and another one in he thing when I had the chance. Stupid white man. All pouf pouf with he big belly and he red face. Is so when you play great. He forget he just the Govna and he think he God. Sending the poor man to he grave. The poor reverend. And him not yet thirty. Is so Govna stay. He always want to make you crawl on you belly so he could play great. Of all the men in this blasted colony, he want to play great with me. Is so all the buckra stay. They will take down they pants and have it with any black skirt what catch they eye and then they goin' turn round and start cussing you for being black. That man treat me like animal all these years. All these years a scrubbing the steps and first shout he hear of we taking we freedom the King give we and he want to kick me in the behind. Me, the woman who serve he all these years.

56

Who give he strong pickney? Doan mind he never take them up. I goin' do for he.

Is not for nothing I is the midwife in this place. Is I who in control of this colony. I know everything going on. When the women can't stand the pain and they don't want belly, is I who go to the bush and find the herbs to quench it. Is I who Celie, Agatha, Princess, and all of them, come to when they sick or when they want play sick. Is I. And all the overseers with their whips can't make them do the field work if I don't give the go-ahead. I telling you. Is who take the rat's vein and boil it for the pickney colic. Is who stop Ol' Haig from taking off Charlotte's skin when she sleeping. Is who take the pepper and the salt to do it with. Is who? But he want play great. Every blasted day he and me in he bedroom for donkeys years. And is Auntie Lou this and is Auntie Lou that. But when push come to shove, he can't even tell me what the King say. He got he freedom. He born with it. But he gotta lie to us. In he prissy prissy voice he gotta say, "Auntie Lou. King say female slaves will not be beaten by the whip…"

I shoulda take a horse whip and beat he then. Blasted white man. He gotta lie to us. To me who serve he umpteen years. He think we blind. But he the one that blind. He blind bad bad. Is do I goin' do for he. God is God. If you wanta play God you goin' suffer. Like dead Massa Reverend John. Like dead Quamina. Govna… You in dead yet. You pack you bags and you gone to Englan'. You think you safe. But as God is my witness, you gone sorry you ever born. You think you safe. You think you goin' leave we here. So so. But you wrong. You wrong.

★ ★ ★ ★ ★

Auntie Lou had not taken long in becoming Auntie Lou. It was a position she cherished almost as much as the hundreds of children she had brought into the world. In her fifty-eight years she had seen much of the inner workings of the colony and of plantation life in general.

Without a father to lay claim to, she came to rely entirely on her mother, whom she resembled to a great degree. But her mother was dead. She was not. Auntie Lou was fat, not a slovenly fat, which only in later years slurred her movements; her fat was energetic, agile, and her body was marked by dimples in her round cheeks and arms. Even in her twenties, the title of Auntie had been given to her by the slaves on the plantation. The buckras had adopted it, finding her a force they thought they could exploit to their own ends. If a slave ran away you could be sure that Auntie Lou would know the whys, the wherefores, and the hows. She settled marital disputes. The women, in particular, came to her with their problems. She had been shunted around from plantation to plantation, bought and sold and bought again until Governor Murrain took up his post in the colony. That was many years ago. The Governor was green, always down with one fever or another. She would see him walking around the slave quarters – inspecting they said. But she knew what he was searching for. He was searching for her. After each of these tours, one of the slave women would work in the big house for a week. It was always one week. The women would be pretty and docile. After that week they would find themselves doing more work on the plantation.

One morning, she was interrupted by loud voices, hands knocking on her door and strained faces. Immediately she gathered up a selection of herbs, clean cloths and a large basin, the tools of her midwife trade. Another baby was about to be born, another woman had to be coaxed into birthing, another umbilical cord had to be cut. But it wasn't a birth. Aggie had come to tell her that her man, Samuel, with whom she had lived for eight years and whom she had borne as many children, was about to be sold.

Aggie was one of the pretty women who had spent a week in the Governor's house before being turned out to work in the fields. Auntie Lou quieted her as best she could, and decided to speak to the Governor on Aggie's behalf. Without changing from her nightdress, she walked over to the main house. As she climbed the steps which opened up onto the wide semi-circle of a verandah, she saw the Governor sitting in his rocking chair, his head nodding gently with its movement, and her anger slowly dissipated as she watched him gradually awaken to her presence. Aggie, Samuel and a few others had gathered round the bottom of the steps. The Governor opened his eyes to a statuesque woman as black as ebony standing before him.

"You have a good sleep, Massa Govna?"

"What in the dickens name are you doing here? Who are you? What are they doing here?" He pointed to the slaves staring up at him.

"I tell you all to go away."

Reluctantly the group left.

The Governor shook himself. "How dare you, woman, come and speak to me at this time of the morning?" He glanced at his timepiece.

"I is Auntie Lou, sah. You know me, sah. I is the midwife on this plantation."

"And so what?"

Auntie Lou clapped her hands twice. A house slave came to the verandah.

"Bring a cool drink for Massa Govna," she directed. She turned to him. "Aggie say you want sell Samuel today, today, sah, Massa Govna sah."

"And what is that to you?"

The slave brandished a tray with a tall glass of rum on it. Auntie Lou took the glass from him and without pausing in her speech, placed it to the Governor's lips.

"Drink this, sah. It goin' wake you up good good."

Without thinking, the Governor drank the contents of the glass. Auntie Lou straightened her body and walked to the rails of the verandah. Feeling Murrain's eyes on her, she turned, knelt on the floor and knee-walked towards him. Kneeling beside him she dabbed his mouth.

"What are you doing? Stop this nonsense... what?"

"I only helping you, sah. Don't sell Samuel, please sah."

"And why ever not?" He was beginning to think this was a dream. But not such a bad one.

"The two o' them... Samuel and Aggie been on this plantation for eight years. Don't break Aggie heart, sah."

The woman was still in her nightdress – a clinging and revealing one.

"Alright. Alright. No need for a sale. But Samuel was a gift really, to Pearsons." He checked himself.

"Thank you, sah. Massa Govna, thank you. God go bless you, sah. You is the best Governor, sah. Thank you, sah, Massa Governor sah."

If he had looked into her eyes, he would have seen they were cold. But he did not.

Any who had doubted Auntie Lou's powers of persuasion were instantly converted. There was dancing and drumming throughout the night as the slaves gave thanks. Governor Murrain had a new sense of himself, as the presents of plantains, yams, and even some hens, were daily placed on his verandah. Auntie Lou's eyes remained cold. Months passed, and the slaves settled down to their daily lives of cutting the cane, boiling sugar or, in Auntie Lou's case, coaxing new life into this world. She was also the object of the Governor's frequent summons for her to come to the house. His arrogance she found tiresome, but it made her strong.

* * * * *

It was only a matter of time before Governor Murrain did what was necessary to install Auntie Lou into the main house proper. She had expected it and was not surprised at the muffled knock on the door of her cabin, the large pendulous form beckoning and the hesitant smile. He could easily have sent one of his house slaves to fetch her, but the Governor had come to her as a man in need of a woman. She returned his smile. Over the years the two developed a relationship which many a husband and wife would have craved. The ritual of silences, conversation, the touching of flesh with flesh, the sharing of moods. Murrain had even shown Auntie Lou his chamber pot. This was no ordinary vessel. Made of fine white porcelain and despite its function, delicate, it was regarded as an heirloom in the Murrain family. Legend had it that the esteemed makers of fine dishes, tureens and soup bowls had delivered a set of these to the lady of the house who promptly placed them on a large dining table, much to the amusement of Lord Murrain, who had mistaken their purpose. His lordship was, indeed, none too refined in his delight in the more crude aspects of the physical. He would, whatever the company, to Lady Murrain's horror, belch, pass wind, and even – in his cups – pee in his pants. Lady Murrain, seeing the possibilities of both pleasing her husband and curbing his more disgusting habits, had commissioned the porcelain makers to use their good services in the creation of a chamber pot for his lordship.

Governor Murrain felt a filial affection for the chamber pot, and when he was appointed Governor, it was one of the first items he had packed. It was thus inevitable that any relationship he had – even if it was with a slave – would have to acknowledge this particular heirloom. Auntie had smiled, seeing in the Governor the man.

And it was for the man that she submitted to the scrubbing of the wooden stairs that led to the door of the Governor's mansion. Other slaves could have done the work with greater ease, but the man in him wanted Auntie Lou to scrub those stairs while he could absorb her every movement. She told herself it was the only thing she would allow herself to give him. It was for Aggie and for the relative freedom the Governor's slaves enjoyed on the plantation. It would provide a platform for the liberty to come.

* * * *

When Auntie Lou scrubs the stairs it is a communion with the wood. She lifts her skirts and petticoats and rests her knees on a cloth pad. Beside her is a bucket loud with the splash of water. With a brush she vigorously scrubs the stairs. Seen from behind, she appears as a bundle of material, folds upon folds of calico. Her soles are parched but her ankles black and shiny with the water. Governor Murrain watches her, and his flesh tingles. He touches his nose. He furtively peeps above the newspaper he is reading and rocks himself to and fro as he unconsciously mimics the movements of the scrubbing brush.

Auntie Lou is aware of his watching. She has two more steps left. She raises an arm to mop at the sweat now pouring from her face. Standing on tip-toe, she throws the contents of the bucket down the stairs. The water gushes out through the gaps onto the grass.

"Be careful, Auntie Lou. Not young any more. . . what?"

She smiles. For years he has been saying the same words. Cradling her skirt about her, she reaches for a pile of old cloths and ties them to a pole and begins to wipe each step in slow succession. The sun shines brightly and she pauses at the bottom of the stairs, shielding her eyes. She waits and he waits for the stairs to dry. When they are, she reaches for a bunch of coconut fibres and dips it into a pot of polish. Then, with a cloth, she begins the process of shining each step, one by one, until she again arrives at the top, breathless.

This is the moment the Governor has been waiting for. He folds his newspaper with deliberation and ambles his way into the silent house. His slaves have been given strict instructions concerning this time of day. Auntie walks behind him to his room, deep in the recesses of the house. It is dominated by a vast four-poster bed above which is a triangular fixture attached to the ceiling from which a flat board hangs, draped with mosquito nets.

There is a dressing table facing the bed made of a dark, rich, shining wood with brass knobs on the drawers; its four legs, like the legs of the four-poster bed, are carved in rivulets of wood that funnel down into the cramped toes of some fanciful wild beast. Films of lacy material adorn it and a square-shaped mirror reflects the room's dark sobriety. A comb and a brush, the comb clinging to the bristles of the brush, nest in one corner of the table. On either side of the only window, heavy curtains, the colour of musty ochre, are restrained from swinging idly by a loop of tasselled rope. Everything in the chamber has a gloomy, subdued elegance. Even the porcelain chamber pot, its sides decorated with pale yellow flowers, its sloping lid rimmed with brass, has dignity.

Auntie stands by the bed. Her garments are wet and her feet have left soft watery footprints. She watches as the Governor removes his morning coat and stands before her in all his corpulence. He slowly undoes the buttons of his shirt. He unsnaps his braces and his trousers fall to the floor. He is now naked, except for a pair of white undershorts (from which she can see sprouting tufts of hair escaping), and his boots. Hair, which his head is denied, grows profusely on his chest and on his arms and legs. His face is a mask of seriousness as Auntie squats massively at his feet. He holds out his right leg, bootedly severe, and she pulls off the boot. Then, steadying himself on the bedrail, he stretches out his left leg. She takes off his other boot. The ritual never changes. He never holds the left foot out first. It is always right followed by left. Her fingers, coarse with hard work, are nevertheless delicate in the way they unlace the boots before placing them beside the chamber pot. The boots now slump, looking strangely abandoned, as if they yearn to contain the man's feet. And not just any feet. The Governor's feet. Governor Murrain's feet.

Auntie Lou stands up abruptly. The house, as always at this time, is silent; the room regards them with all the dignity it can muster. Auntie Lou resumes her position by the bed, her hands resting on the hard woodenness of its four-postered frame. It is a heavy, hard wood, and in some forgotten time past, slaves had transported it to the plantation. Other slaves had sawed it, hammered in the nails… with hands wet with sweat. The Governor's feet are soft and white, the toenails thin, flimsy. They curve in the shape of the boots.

Auntie Lou bends forward slowly and removes the lid of the chamber pot. The Governor straddles over the vessel and a stream of yellow liquid arches into the pot. The Governor's eyes interlock with Auntie Lou's. She closes the lid of the pot, and holding it carefully takes it out of the room and as carefully places it down beside the door. She shuts the door fast. The Governor, his face a picture of cherubic innocence, stretches his full length on the rich covers of the bed and falls soundly asleep.

* * * * *

The forest is quiet with white light. The fresh-turned earth is raw on John's grave. Auntie Lou looks at the fallen Bible.

"God! God! Is what you do here in Demerara? Is what? God, you gotta plan for we, you pickney? I can't deny it. I angry with you. Why you allow John, you own fellow down here, to die? We blind, but you got eye. All o' we blind in the end. John dead. You couldn't wait for the pardon from the King to come through before he dead? Is what wrong with you? Quamina dead and he smelling up the place too bad. Why you does give us crosses to bear when you know we can't bear them? Is why?

"I telling you, God, whether I right or I wrong, whether I go to bottom or top, I going make sure Govna don't meet England. Why you make them so blind? You make a garden out here for we. We got flower and nice thing . . . then you bring in the snake… What for? You having fun up there? You laughing at we? You laughing to see the thing we does call revolt? Laugh again, God. Go ahead and laugh you big belly laugh.

"Look at me, God. Look at me. I telling you, if is revolt you looking for, you going see. This Demerara going be free. An ah going kill for it. And ah going birth so many pickney them, you going see. You hearing me, God? You listening to me? Listen good.

"And as for you, Govna, is sleep you sleep. Is I make you sleep. You turn 'gainst me. I, the woman who see you piss in the pot and make you forget you the Govna. You in know is I who give you the brave for piss. It in natural. You is a man…You don't know that when you piss,

I know you. I know the Govna. I know the King. I know all the buckra them when you piss. I know they does piss. I know where the piss come from. I see it with me two eye. I not blind. Baby born and a' them can't see. I see. I know. That is why I could talk talk with the men them. You does pass wind. It smell. You does belch. You like women them. You like me. But I know. You does piss…and every time I see you piss I get strong, man. I get strong. Woman get strong. You in going piss in London. In England you in going piss. Like you piss on we with your control of we, I gon fix you piss."

★ ★ ★ ★ ★

"Do you feel stronger now?" It's that hospital nurse again. "You can stop using that bed pan, M'am. . ."

She holds me by the shoulders. Although I have not been lying in bed that long, my legs feel stiff and I grimace. The nurse notices my distress and increases her hold. She manoeuvres me to the bathroom. She even helps me sit on the toilet seat. I wonder if *she* feels strong when she helps me in this most basic of needs. She tells me that I can go home and I'm so happy when the ambulance drops me there. The entire household is there, including Gardener and Nurse's mother. They are all delighted to see me. Nurse's mother is particularly delighted, so much so that she accompanies me to my bedroom. To escape I go to the bathroom and close the door. I am sitting on the loo seat when she walks in. She does not, as one would expect, apologize and immediately go away. She stands there, looks at me and only then says, "Sorry darling." In my own house I am sweetie and I am darling. She does not stop talking. "How is the pregnancy coming along?"

"Close the door!" I shout at her. I flush the toilet and come out into the bedroom.

She is sitting on the bed. She evidently thinks that because her daughter is now in our employ we are one big family. Before I can decide how to handle the situation, my little daughter runs in. Mercifully, she is without her nursery rhyme book. I am up to my neck in Georgie Porgies, Little Miss Muffets and Humpty Dumpties. When this next child is born I shall be a walking nursery rhyme with some fairy tales thrown in for good measure. My daughter starts playing with mother of Nurse.

"You know, I was thinking… wouldn't it be nice for you to have your new baby at home instead of in that dreadful hospital?"

"Hospitals serve their purpose," I snap.

She does not seem offended. "Of course they do. But I was thinking that if you ever wanted a midwife, I'd be glad to help out."

My daughter squirms. "Mummy, wee wee. I want to wee."

"Two years old and not properly potty trained! She should be able to go to the potty by herself."

She is attacking the essence of my motherhood. "I don't believe in forcing children," I say. She is unperturbed and takes my daughter to the bathroom and straddles her over the tiny children's toilet.

"I'm glad you've decided to take Nurse's fiancé as your steward. You need as much help as you can get. We don't want any more near miscarriages, do we?" says Mother of Nurse. No we do not. There will be no miscarriage of any kind, whether of baby, child, or of justice. The C word, the first of my creating word-worlds, has taken care of that.

She leaves with my daughter and my husband comes in; he looks beautiful as only a man who is under the control of God can look beautiful. His face shines and my heart beats with love. Is it so wrong, so unchristian to want some of that love for myself?

"When was the last time I told you that I loved you?"

"When you proposed." He laughs and sits beside me, holding my hand.

"Now that you're so busy preaching the Word of God and saving the nation through the Outreach, you're just, oh I don't know... You love so many people now, you have so many brothers and sisters in Christ you have no time left for me."

He is serious. "Why do you continue to upset yourself with such thoughts? Ever since you began writing your novel... I love God and I love you. You are a part of me."

"Why? Because God says so?"

"Don't you know that God made us one, that we are a single unit in his eyes?"

"That's probably why it was you who went through a near miscarriage." The words escape my mouth. "You spend your time at work. Then you come home and bury yourself in your Bible. Then you go to a fellowship. When you return, you go to sleep. And I, I am left alone."

I think immediately that I should not be saying this. I recall the fairy tale which tells of a princess who, through the actions of her wicked mother-in-law, has lost her baby. The princess is told that if she wants to keep the new baby she carries, she has to stay silent. When she can no longer suppress the urge to speak, she slips out of the castle at dead of night, tears up turf, digs into the raw earth with her crazy sacrificial fingers and makes a long tunnel. She sticks her head into the hole and screams her heart out; then she seals the hole back with the turf she has ripped up.

"Look, I didn't mean to upset you. God is with you. He is with us. He is in control of us."

"Are you sure?"

"Why, my dear, of course I'm sure. All will be well. Read your Bible. Pray. Look at how I've changed."

And he has, as he said, changed. He is in Christ a new creature. I shall think only of creation and try not to feel so shut out of this transforming, wonderful gift of his life in Christ. It shall be mine, too. It is a gift freely given. Not so free.

"Are you going to Bible class this evening?"

He is silent. "Yes, I'm going; why don't you come with me?"

"You're going? Nurse must stay here. She isn't going with you."

"If you insist," he says.

"I do. I very much do."

I shall spend the entire night writing and I shall not go down to tea, especially if there is Demerara sugar anywhere in the house. I shall write PART TWO. I have exposed the demons with my words and it is now time to kill. But before I can begin to write anything at all, I hear a commotion downstairs. I come down and in the living room are soldiers with heavy guns and heavy black boots marking my floor. There are no introductions. They push my husband aside roughly. One of them, in deference to my pregnant state, tells me to sit down. Then the rat-a-tat barking begins. The fangs drip fat boils of saliva and I watch them drop.

"So you are a writer?"

"Yes." I have learnt to be careful with words.

"What do you want with us?" asks my husband.

"Shut up!" Another bark.

"What are you writing?"

"I'm writing a novel about the last slave insurrection which took place in my homeland, Guyana, in 1823. It concerns. . ."

"Are you writing anything about Nigeria, about that traitor who called himself a poet?"

"No."

"Bring am. Bring your paper."

I show him my sheaves of papers and he reads in an appropriate sing-song voice. "Three blind mice. Three blind mice."

His laughter convulses him so much that his uniform jiggles. My husband offers them beer and after they have drunk they leave, on their lips that simple nursery rhyme. Three blind mice. I am grateful for nursery rhymes, for the hangings of Cs and Os, especially for a special C. And I draw, draw in the obscure regions of Demerara, of Nigeria; I draw in hope of the marvellous light of a sought-for freedom; I draw:

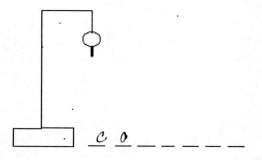

Well, well… if that drawing is a bit wobbly, you'll have to excuse me. Peace of mind needed. Let me see… I can't afford to let what happened in Demerara affect my life here in Nigeria. Those soldiers spell danger for me and mine. Dear God, I can't see and see I must. Sometimes I know exactly what's going on. I mean really know-see, and then it's a case of I no-see. See-saw. Up and down. I know that Gardener and Quamina are one and the same, and I know all about that wretched Rosita-ish Nurse of a girl and how she wants to do both Mary and me in, but well… maybe my pregnancy hormones are skidaddling all over the place. Yes, that must be the reason why I'm eye-focused conscious and eye-blind unconscious, out of control and in control all at the same time. And time is of the essence now. It is imperative I get back to the novel and follow the lead of the nursery rhyme which my daughter unwittingly gave me. Let's see how those three blind mice ran... Here goes...

PART TWO

SEE HOW THEY RUN

Well, he, Reverend John Smithers was going to bring them gold. The Blacks. Heathen denied the Word. His brothers in Christ. This was his mission.

His eyes scanned the waves of the ocean rising and falling and he felt the lurching boards of the ship wheeze, creaking with an immense weariness. Mary was in their cabin. She was a good choice of wife. A Christian man with a mission had to have a good wife.

Others had gone to this El Dorado for gold, the dust which gleamed and poisoned their minds, but he would discover his own El Dorado. Demerara would never be the same after he had left his mark on the slaves. God's black children with his stigmata biting into their flesh and souls.

A great wall of water had crashed into the ship and he had seen his feet scaling the water and his eyes met the white-crested waves and he had smiled.

Praise God a thousand times. A million times. Who would have thought that he, John Smithers, ordinary John Smithers, would have had this opportunity to bring the light of God to the slaves in Demerara? Who would have thought it? His labours had not been in vain. Demerara beckoned. He could hardly wait to begin God's work and his.

He felt alive with memory. The travelling to this road had not been easy. His mind traversed the narrow cobbled lanes; the gangs of boys pilfering cabbages and bread; sleeping under bridges; the freezing cold winters which entered his chest and his lungs with a wracking cough that had never left him… Any notion of God had been forgotten in that time and his mouth rounded on the inward words: "May God forgive me for my sinful pleasures. The sin of sour wine, the sin of Margaret and Jennifer and Lorraine. My wicked heart. My ungodly heart. May God forgive me."

And he had been forgiven, and now this escape to a God-given land, Demerara. It was a chance to begin again and conquer black souls, and perhaps his own.

Three sea birds knifed the sky's emptiness and their wings cut their raw edges into his heart. He must not be superstitious. Superstition was for the illiterate. The godless. He was now a learned man, versed in the Bible and the classics. Why, then, this nagging? Were the three birds a sign from God? Three. Three crosses. The cock crowed thrice and Christ was betrayed. Life would not betray him. God had given him this chance. God would not, could not betray him. Reverend Jones the preacher had made sure of that. Look at the name of the chapel into which he wandered. Silver Street Chapel. Silver. Gold. He had passed through silver and now there was only the gold of souls to be grasped. The fourth commandment was being read as he entered the chapel. It was no accident.

"Yes, my conscience smote me. I was and am convinced of sin. I am a sinner. Blessed be God. That conviction shall never leave me."

A sailor joined him. "Rev, not talking to yourself are ye?"

"Only thinking aloud."

The sailor stared at the tall figure, the red hair tousled by the wind. But that hadn't been it. The travelling had continued in his roaming feet and his heart, which could find no anchoring rest. How could God accept him with his many, many sins? He would never forget that year, 1810. He had been adrift in a maze of words until Isaiah sliced straight to his heart. "Seek the Lord while He may be found; call ye upon Him while He is near. Let the wicked forsake his way, and the unrighteous man his thoughts, and let him return unto the Lord, and He will have mercy upon him, and to our God, for He will abundantly pardon."

He will abundantly pardon. God is merciful. When we reach Demerara, I shall abundantly pardon. Poor sweet black children. They knew no better than to pursue a heathenish existence. May God help them and me.

But God hadn't finished with him. He chuckled; the sailor stared. God had not only embraced his soul. He had clutched at his body. There hadn't been a lull in those entire eleven weeks. Day after day the fever had raged, his flesh seemingly bitten by tiny love bites. He'd thought he was going to die. Isaiah was wrong. God had betrayed him. The fever had been a hot blanket of fire which daily smothered him with the heat of passionate kisses. His new companions had said that anyone suffering from such an attack of smallpox would never recover. When they left his sick bed it was with furrows on their brows. "At last, John is suffering for his wayward ways." They had prayed. John had prayed, but it was more like an argument. "God," said his worn flesh, "save me. If you help me, if you make me recover, then I will devote my love to you, my life." The fever ebbed. The flesh had resumed its pallid smoothness and again John was travelling to make heaven his home.

God-Isaiahed, looking over his shoulder, he had attended church regularly, felt the power of God within him. It was a miracle. Proudly he had told Mary, "I am in Christ a new creature; old things have passed away; all things have become new."

Mary had just tossed her hair and remained silent. Perhaps she was too struck by the enormity of his conviction to respond. In a mission such as his it was important to have an able, pious woman by his side. Reverend Neweley had said so. He wondered how his old friend was. He had helped so much. It was a debt that could not be repaid: introducing him to music, the classics, and of course his beloved Bible. Above all, his old friend had no reservations in helping him to this appointment as the missionary for Demerara.

And then that envelope from Rev. Wray, the Pastor of Bethel Chapel at Le Resouvenir estate… Must be approaching eighty by now. After a lifetime of service to God in the colonies, the man wanted to return to England. He, John Smithers, would be the new pastor. England was behind. Before him was Demerara. Those etchings of the landscape of Demerara, its flowers, birds, its fish. He had never seen such a large fish before, even in a picture – except Jonah's whale. He was no Jonah but he would, Isaiah in him, bring salvation to the blacks. Even now he felt the letter of appointment in his hands.

Demerara. Demerary. It sounded like a sweet lullaby on the tongue. As sweet as the sugar the slaves produced. He must have some tea. With plenty of sugar.

The sailor continued to stare at the lone figure on the deck, now rapidly walking, now stopping to steady himself as he made his way back to his wife.

* * * * *

75

The night had been hot; Mary saw their bedchamber through the gauze of mosquito netting and it was as if the fine network of holes was directing her vision.

So this was Demerara. She glanced around to look at John. He was pacing the room. He seemed anxious. He should have been comforting her now, when she most needed him. But no. He would have to be the Reverend John Smithers, wouldn't he?

She tugged at the nightdress which clung to her legs. The heat was unbearable.

"I shall never survive this," she whispered. "How can heat make one so very drained?"

They had been assigned seven slaves. A modest number, the number that their predecessor had permitted himself as a man of the cloth. She tried to stifle a giggle. The cloth, a ring around the neck. Clothes to hide bodies with. They, the reverends, should be men of the flesh letting the love of God shine through their bodies. They should be Adamic, naked. John. My darling John. His first godly act had been to dismiss the slaves.

She saw palm fronds whisking drowsily in the corner of the windows. If he hadn't told the slaves to go, they could have slept comfortably.

"So you're awake, too?" he asked.

"I couldn't sleep. The heat. Don't you feel it?"

"We'll get used to it. There's so much to be done here. I can hardly wait for daylight. Thank heaven Reverend Wray obtained a preaching license for me from the Governor."

She dragged the mosquito net from the bed, ducked under it and joined him looking through the bedroom window. John placed an arm about her waist.

"My goodness, you're soaking with sweat."

"It's so hot," she said and returned to sit on the bed, a bed so high that she could swing her feet from it.

"Well, Mary, what do you think of the place so far?"

So far meant the streets of Georgetown, the houses held high on pillars, canals dimpled by floating lilies, white, purple and deep pink. The bustle of market. The slave women in gaudy cotton prints, striped handkerchiefs on their heads, balancing baskets on top of them. So far... The strong smell of burnt sugar hanging like a thick curtain in the air. The slaves on the auction block at the stelling. So far... the two-tiered structure of the manse of Le Resouvenir Plantation which, resting squarely on pillars, its interior austere and somewhat clinical, looked to her like a small domestic hospital with its white sheets on the bed, and scrubbed floorboards; this was the house where she was to be wife, a missionary's wife.

So far... Meeting with Rev. John Wray, who insisted on showing them around the plantation, exhausted as they were.

"Mary, my dear, I asked you what your impressions of the colony were so far."

"Indeed you did, John. I didn't care much for Reverend Wray... Well, the way he spoke in figures... Le Resouvenir, he says, is a good eight miles from Georgetown. Forty-nine plantations on the East Coast of Demerara..."

Her voice was mocking. "And Reverend John Smithers, I should be... What did he say? What did he tell you?... Since we British have taken over from the Dutch, the colony has grown enormously. Reverend John Smithers, Quamina, a slave on Plantation Success, wants to show you Bethel Chapel himself. And Reverend John Smithers, the slaves troop to Bethel Chapel from so many plantations and they are more enthusiastic about God than many a colonist. And John, I am so very hot, but I'll go downstairs and prepare breakfast. I saw some eggs and bread in the kitchen yesterday."

"Yes, do that. There's a good wife. I had no idea that your memory was so so... Most encouraging, my dear. It's our first day. We have to make an early start and don't forget we've been invited to the Governor's birthday party this evening. We'll have a chance to meet the gentry of the colony."

Mary washed and dressed slowly and went downstairs to make their morning meal. She thought about that word "dear". Dear Mary. Dear eggs. Dear breakfast. Dear Demerara. Dear wife. She had to try and help John in his work in this godforsaken colony. She placed the dishes on the table. She boiled water and made coffee. The coffee smelt rich and strong. She sat down and drank, enjoying the flavour and its heat running in her body.

John appeared, looking cheerful.

"Splendid. I could eat a horse. I can't explain it... I'm tired and full of vigour at the same time, my dear."

He did not tell her of *his* unease when they were met by Rev. John Wray. The man had indeed arranged a preaching license for him, had even recommended that Quamina be allowed to become the chief deacon in the church. Wray had told him that Quamina had had his brushes with the buckra and had once run away, but that he seemed changed and was now a godfearing Christian and wielded much influence with the slaves. It would be useful to have him on his side.

"Side?"

To which Wray had replied, "It's not easy being a pastor to the slave community. None of our kind attend Bethel Chapel, except Hamilblade, the overseer here – and even he keeps out of the way much of the time. What I'm saying is that you're bound to get some stick from the majority of the plantation owners, the white buckra, as the slaves call us… and perhaps from the Governor himself. He's an amiable sort but, how shall I put it? He has been known to be anti-missionary. The important thing to remember is that you're here to convert the slaves into being good Christians. Laissez-faire is the watchword. Lots of dos and don'ts over here, I'm afraid, but I think you'll find the work rewarding. I don't know to what extent you've been briefed by the directors of the London Missionary Society, but even if you only convert a single one of the slaves and make them, encourage them to attend Bethel Chapel regularly, you will have achieved a great deal." Here Wray had paused. "In your service to King George and the British Empire and to the Big Man himself, Governor Murrain…"

He had interrupted and told Wray that the only Big Man he knew was God. Wray had warned him, most seriously, to hold his tongue and keep his views to himself at the Governor's party.

★ ★ ★ ★ ★

When my husband wakes me up, he tells me I've been sleeping far too long and that I've been locked up in some kind of self-imposed imprisonment, whether in our house or in the hospital, or in my mind, since my friend was hanged... I look at him when he says that and I agree to go for a drive around Lagos. Silently he helps me out of bed.

"I'm OK, really I am. As soon. . ."

"I know, you've told me before. As soon as you finish your book, everything will work out fine. Meanwhile, why don't you put on this dress. . . You look lovely in it."

Nurse has taken our daughter to the shops. As we leave the house I see her betrothed has shears in his hands and is clipping off the heads of flowers, the stems, branches, whatever. Just clipping them off.

"Master, should I drive?"

"No thank you," my husband replies.

We sit in the car and I do have a sensation of freedom, Demerara-less. Seven characters-less.

"Thought I'd take you to old Ikoyi... How's that?"

Old Ikoyi used to be the residential district for the hoi-polloi British colonialists. They lived big and in obvious comfort in sprawling bungalows with houseboys' quarters attached. Some Nigerians still call these flats *boys'* quarters and their adult stewards *boys*, without batting an eyelash.

Wide gardens unravelled in a stream of green lawns; hedges of hibiscus and frangipani trees displayed flowers of creamy yellow, deep pinks and white. Sometimes the heavy scent of the flowers would pounce upon you as if they wanted to frighten you into their beauty. Outside these houses the relatives of the servants have established businesses – tables selling an assortment of cigarettes, kola nuts, sweets, toilet tissue, mosquito coils, tomato puree in red shiny tins, tinned milk, blue boxes of cubed sugar, bottles of groundnuts, dark green bars of soap, candles, matches and salt in small parcels of plastic.

"Let's go to Ajegunle or Mushin where the real people live and please, when we get there, I want you to turn off the air-conditioner."

"Whatever for?" he asks, but my face bullies him into moving the car onto the Third Mainland Bridge. We are leaving genteel Ikoyi and Victoria Island, named after the British Queen Victoria. The bridge is long. I close my eyes, trying not to think. Even though my eyes are closed, I know when we get to Mushin. I can smell the heavy stench of poverty.

"Why you want to upset yourself continually, I do not know," my husband says almost inaudibly. I do not tell him with the blunt edges of my mouth that it is very important for me never to forget what Butcher Boy is doing, has done and will continue to do, unless we stop him.

"I'm going to close the windows," my husband says.

He shuts out the stench of rot, decay, the foul smell of unwashed human beings; limbs stuck to limbs lounging beside stacks of rubbish; the open gutters of defecation and the slap-stick hovels; the studied chewing of a chewing-stick by a man whose wrapper of sleep is held up by a rope which tries to hide his distended, amala starch-filled belly; the woman who stirs and stirs a cooking pot of frying oil in which swim wedges of yam and sweet potato before they are lifted up in long iron spoons and strained of oil and placed in newspaper to sell to the few who have managed to get work.

"Satisfied?" my husband asks as he sees me ready to cry.

"Let's go home now."

But we can't because we're surrounded by a bunch of beggars. We should not have stopped the car, even for a moment. It's too late to do anything. Most of the beggars have missing limbs and at least two of them are attached to children who hold tin pots to collect money. They surround the car and a sing-song kind of litany starts to sound in my head. I'm afraid when I hear them.

"Oga, give us something now."

"You be Butcher Boy friend, no?"

"I beg we never eat since…"

"Oga help us, oh."

The words glue together in a vast mouth of begging and they push, rock the car backwards and forwards.

"Get out, you people!"

We've been "rescued" by some soldiers. It is a rescue of a sort only because, as the beggars disappear, melting away from view, they have been replaced, almost to a man, by more soldiers – who seem to have a flair for multiplication ever since Nigeria gained her independence from the British some thirty odd years ago.

"It is good, Oga, that we could help you."

"Na wa for this country-oh!"

"Oga, give us something-oh!"

They tell us what we know already. That Butcher Boy will not be happy to learn that his officers have saved an oyinbo dudu and her husband without giving them something.

When we are on the Third Mainland Bridge again, heading for Ikoyi, I feel hemmed in by present and past; by country and country. I look at my dress and I'm still thinking of hemming. It's supposed to be a tidying up, a neatening of the raw seams and seamy side of life. Hem. Hem.

"What are you saying hem hem for?"

"I'm tired. I want to go home."

"We are going home. I'm sorry about the beggars," he says. We pass Falomo. Butcher Boy is reputed to have bought this gigantic shopping centre and the Law Buildings, plus he's got millions of the country's money stashed away in foreign banks.

"What are you thinking about? What's on your mind now? Are you OK?"

"Of course I'm OK," I snap, and then I'm sorry and I say in a nicer voice, "Of course I'm OK."

"God is quite capable of handling the affairs of this country, you know. . ."

"Did I say He wasn't? But when in the name of Jesus is this injustice going to stop? When are we going to be free? I don't mean just democratically free? I mean free, really free."

"Sweetie, I love you," he says as we turn into Victoria Island. Modern businesses and, recently, a plethora of banks have burgeoned in this area. Big banks. Middle-sized banks and little banks everywhere.

"I too am banking on God to set us free," I say. "No one else has been able to do it."

He smiles. "I agree with you. Leave it to Him. Do your part in praying and…"

"That hanging of my friend."

"Don't bring that up again; you seem determined to upset yourself. Be positive."

"You don't understand," I tell him. "The hanging is a positive thing. I really believe so."

I can see he thinks I'm going to talk about the Hangman's Game, and even the profile of his face, the downward slant of his intelligent-looking nose, his forehead and the strong firm neck on the supportive shoulders and the shirt of blue and the trousers and the fashionable belt with its buckle are all thinking that I'm going to mention the Hangman's Game in relation to Butcher Boy's antics and my dead poet. The profile of his face is the first to speak, it remains a profile, an outline saying, "Please sweetie, don't do this to yourself. God has everything under His control. Stop these thoughts or you'll kill yourself."

Something like that… the profile, ever so profile, says. Then it attempts to flesh out.

"I've got something which should interest you. We're invited to a party at the President's."

"Why? We're just a pastor and his oyinbo dudu writer wife."

"I think old Butcher Boy might see us both as a threat… I don't know."

So a bunch of cut-throats, elitist cut-throats, have invited us to a dinner at State House. I should say hang-throats not cut-throats. It should be interesting to see what hang-throats eat for dinner. It cannot be normal fare.

"Feeling guilty after the hanging is he… El Presidente? Butcher Boy?"

★ ★ ★ ★ ★

Like most of the great houses which chequered the slave plantations of the well-to-do, the Governor's mansion stood erect, many-roomed and wide-girthed in the centre of a lawn of well-mannered green grass. An imposing presence, with painted white wooden exterior supported by elegant yet sturdy pillars, it rose in haughty grandeur as if impervious to the ravaging seas swelling around the sunken coast of Georgetown, and the swelling discontent of black slave labour on the land. Through numerous latticed windows thrust open by white wooden stakes, it surveyed the rambling gardens and sugar cane fields beyond. Leading up to it was a long gravel path lined by a hibiscus hedge of bright red flowers, with filaments springing from their open mouths.

After being checked by guardsmen resplendent in their Governor's livery, after walking or driving up the path, visitors to the mansion would see well-polished brown steps which led to a wide verandah. On this stood small circular white tables, sets of white rattan chairs with cushions, the colours, red and blue. On the extreme right of the verandah was the Governor's rocking chair, which even now stirred with the motion of its occupant, His Excellency Governor Theophilus Edward George Murrain of the colony of Demerara.

"This house resembles a wedding cake," Mary murmured as the Smithers climbed the steps up to the verandah. There, Mary grasped the outstretched hand of the Governor.

A fat black woman hovered by the door, her form eclipsing those of the sentries. She introduced herself as Auntie Lou.

"Don't know what I'd do without her," the Governor boomed. "Well-polished steps, what?"

"I shine them good for my Massa Govna."

"Auntie Lou does everything for me. Won't allow any of the other slaves to touch the steps." The Governor was expansive.

Auntie Lou shuffled around the verandah arranging this wicker chair, that small table. She walked to the banisters, shaded her eyes and announced, "Massa Govna, they no come out yet. I did tell you pre-dinner, or whatever you want to call it, not a good idea. But it always the same with you and..."

The Governor noted the surprise in Mary's expression and with a hoarseness in his tone said, "You'd better go, Auntie Lou, and... go and get us some refreshment."

She swept up her skirts and mumbled her way into the house, scarcely acknowledging the presence of the sentries who stood rigid as statues.

"Don't know what I'd do without her. Good woman. Better slave..." he laughed. "Been together... What will you have to drink, Reverend Smithers, Mrs. Smithers? What will you have to drink? I always have a good rum myself. Rum and coconut water; best drink in the world, what? But I suppose you being a reverend and all...Well... What'll you have? What'll you have?"

"Coconut water will be fine on its own, thank you."

John nodded agreement just as a girl tiptoed onto the verandah, balancing a tray with cat-like grace.

"Excellent, excellent, Rosita."

The girl stood behind John Smithers' chair.

"It's very good, very good," continued the Governor, "that I have you to myself before the other guests arrive. Reverend Wray told me about your arrival, of course. Good man. Understands the workings of a slave colony. And my boy, you need to...Wanted the Pearsons and Gruegels and Captain McTurkeyen to be here ... but never mind, never mind."

Mary took in the evening sky, a stretch of mellowing pink against which palm trees, like dark-leaved stars, swayed on poles. The entire garden seemed to be preparing for its night's rest; the hibiscus flowers closing their petals, the grass no longer the iridescent green of hot day. The Governor noted her gaze.

"Best garden in the world, what? Had a mango tree in that corner," he pointed vaguely. "And two paw paw trees. Had them cut down. Two many of those pickaninnies climbing over them. Too much bother."

Birds on their way home veed in perfect baseless triangles, as if spearheading some secret mission.

Ladybird, ladybird fly away home, your house is empty. Your children gone.

"Are those ladybirds?" Mary asked, pointing.

"Ladybirds? Gentlemen birds perhaps, what? Er... Lovely gown you're wearing. I can see you've just arrived in Demerara. Not easy keeping things white out here." And the Governor guffawed as Mary looked at her best white satin skirt.

"My goodness, the Pearsons and the Gruegels are late. You can always trust the Gruegels to be late. Dutch, you know. They own one of the most prosperous plantations in the colony... Vryheids Lust. But the Pearsons... British you know. Can't think what's holding them up. McTurkeyen's late too. Reverend Smithers, yes... Demerara is over-powering."

John managed a smile and the Governor turned his head as Auntie Lou reappeared and touched his shoulder, whispering, "Rosita."

"Ah yes! Rosita."

The girl curtsied as if she had been waiting for this moment.

"This is Rosita," the Governor boomed. "Auntie Lou's daughter. You could have her as your personal slave. Good girl. Hard working. Very Christian. Understand you got rid of your house slaves upon arrival, what?"

"I, we, Mary and I don't believe in having servants. God has said that everyone is His servant, His slave and..."

The Governor winced. "Well, Wray did warn me... Mr. Smithers, what exactly is your purpose here? Why have you come to this colony?"

"To attend this dinner party, Your Excellency. Happy Birthday, Governor Murrain."

Mary spoke in a steady trot and Governor Murrain's facial muscles relaxed.

"Well what about it?"

"What about what, Sir?" asked John.

"What about having Rosita as your servant, slave – the terminology does not matter. Your wife will need some help about the house. Someone to show her the ropes, what?"

Rosita, who had been standing still, her eyes fixed on the floor, raised her head and looked directly into John's eyes. She saw their blue-grey earnestness. She saw the firm jaw, the neck clothed in

85

rounds of white cloth in a stylish cravat; she saw the aquiline nose, the face so lean and ascetic it made her want to reach out and touch. She saw the burnished red of fiery orange hair moving rebelliously over a white forehead and she looked away, enchanted.

John was the first to speak. To be tempted so soon. "If you insist, Sir."

Rosita, in a half-walk, half-run, vanished into the house.

"That's settled then," said the Governor. "Taking our quinine are we?"

"Yes sir. We have taken our quinine. But there are not many mosquitoes at Le Resouvenir."

"God keeping them away from his select few, is he? His special slaves and servants, what?"

"I did not say so, Sir."

"Mosquitoes everywhere, my man. Always make sure you and the little woman use your net."

"Yes sir."

The Governor adjusted his frame in the rocking chair. "Got along well with Wray. Good chap. Never gave me, us, any trouble whatsoever. Hope I'll have the same relationship with you, Smithers."

"I don't think I quite understand your meaning, Sir."

"Course you do."

The Governor turned his attention to Mary. "He, your husband understands, doesn't he, my good woman?"

"Sir, your Excellency, I don't mean to offend you," John began.

"Of course you don't. My mother had red hair."

"Sir?"

"Temperamental people. Use the Good Book to keep yourself in check, what? In control?"

"Sir, I intend to do my mission, to accomplish God's mission here to the best of my ability."

The Governor ceased rocking, frowned, placed his hands on his thighs and regarded his tightly-laced boots. "That's what I was afraid of, Smithers. On no account must you do your best. You'll find, my boy, that doing your best is the wrong policy to pursue out here. You have to remember that blacks are not like you and me. The black is a different species altogether. Sons of Ham, what? That's why they're black. Black as sin. The blacks are here to work. God created the leaders and the led. The blacks are to be led. Why is it that they are slaves and we are not?"

"I believe, Governor Murrain, that we, mankind, created slavery. God provides us with liberation as He did with the Israelites of old and when He sent His son Jesus Christ to die for us that was... that was..."

"It is God who ordained things like this, Smithers; if God did not approve of slavery, it would not exist."

Auntie Lou's head appeared around the door. "Massa Govna, I tell you to take things easy easy or you going to get..."

The Governor, had he been younger and more agile, might have risen and even struck Auntie Lou. As it was, he sat in his rocking chair rocking violently as she disappeared.

"On no account," he addressed John, "on no account must you do your best. You can help us and the slaves by making them enjoy their work. Promise them only that heaven is good and they'll get there if they obey their masters. That sort of thing."

But Smithers refused to acknowledge the warning signals of anger driving through his head or Mary's pouting lips.

"Your Excellency, I intend to do my duty here as pastor to the slaves, as a servant of God."

The Governor clenched the armrests of his rocking chair.

"Let me, in turn be plain with you, Mr. Smithers. Any talk of a white man as a servant, as a servant to anyone; any talk of anything which smells of possible slave revolt and I'll send you packing! Is that clear? I could do with another toddy of rum. Best drink in the world, what?"

He clapped his hands and Rosita came out and poured him rum and coconut water. When she'd done this she stood behind John yet again. Murrain regarded Mary, who sat silently, cupping her glass in her hands.

"You would do well, Mr. Smithers, to follow the example of your little woman. Listen to me very carefully, Smithers. I, as Governor of this colony, will not permit any change in the regulations, Christianity or no Christianity, God or no God."

"The regulations?"

"The regulations that apply to servants and masters."

"I am aware of them..."

A clatter of horses' hooves cut across Smithers' words, and glancing at the driveway, he saw two carriages approaching the

Governor's house and in the distance a lone figure rapidly galloping on horseback. The occupants of the carriages, the Pearsons and the Gruegels, alighted from their respective vehicles and climbed the stairs to the verandah. The Governor remained seated.

"Thought you were never coming," he declared.

Mrs. Gruegel, in heavily accented English, explained that they had decided to come in one body, but that Captain McTurkeyen had kept them waiting for over an hour. The man in question jumped from his horse and with swift deliberate movements handed the reins to a slave.

"Theo! Sorry to keep you waiting. I'm off into the interior tomorrow as you know... I just got the information of the whereabouts of that runaway..."

"This is Mr. John Smithers and his little woman... taking the place of Wray here as pastor of Bethel Chapel," said the Governor.

The Smithers bowed.

"We've got some time before the other guests arrive. I'm a fair man," the Governor paused as if trying to establish this quality in himself. "Wanted to give this here reverend a chance to discuss what's what in the colony. Got along with Wray; owe it to his successor to be fair."

Captain McTurkeyen nodded in the direction of the doors of the house and the Governor took his cue. "Time for a man-to-man talk. Wouldn't want to corrupt the ears of the womenfolk, what?"

Mrs. Pearsons held out her hand to Mary, who rose and the three women were ushered into the house.

"Off with you, Rosita," cried Governor Murrain. "Get used to your new mistress."

Without a word Rosita complied, following the rustle of skirts.

★ ★ ★ ★ ★

That, I suppose, is that. Mary and John Smithers have met the Demerara hoi polloi and His Excellency the Governor. They've been given Rosita as a house-help and I have John and Mary quarrelling over that after the party. She thinks John is attracted to Rosita because of the way he looks at her. He's so annoyed with what he calls her "unwarranted jealousy" that he wants to get rid of her for the time being and persuades her to accompany Mrs. Pearsons and Mrs. Gruegel into the interior on Captain McTurkeyen's slave-catching expedition. Mary reluctantly agrees but says that Rosita must go with them. As for the Governor and McTurkeyen, they believe John to be a dangerous upstart who is determined to upset the slave system with his talk of teaching the slaves how to read and write, of the sacredness of Sundays for slaves and so on. McTurkeyen... I have to do something about him soon in terms of the plot... Anyway McTurkeyen says that the Governor won't have any real problems with Smithers because he is not the most circumspect of men. Smithers, who hasn't been in the colony for a week, proves his point when he decides to make Quamina, a former runaway, his Chief Deacon.

I think at this point I have it right. Nothing major has happened so far, but I've established that John is capable of losing his temper and incapable of wise silence.

I must do my hair and my nails and my make-up for the dinner party at the President's mansion. I haven't anything to wear except my one and only going-out dress, black and voluminous. I shall look like a huge black tome. My husband is spruce as usual in a suit and cravat. He is reading from his Bible, which is almost as large and as black and as pregnant as my maternity dress.

"What are you reading?" I ask as I comb my hair.

"My Bible of course."

"I know you're reading your Bible, but from which part?"

"I'm reading about betrayal. Hurry up! We don't want to be late. Everyone… the who's who of Lagos will be there."

"Betrayal!"

"Do hurry up!"

I'm staring at him. He will get annoyed if I keep him waiting.

"So you're reading about betrayal?"

"I'm not in the mood for questions."

He is a Man of God. He is not allowed to get angry. Anger is a sin. This thought gives me comfort.

"Will Nurse come along with us?" I ask sweetly.

"Of course not."

So Nurse isn't coming along with us. I shall have my husband to myself.

I am dressed now but I do not look in the mirror.

"Nurse!" I shout.

She materializes. "Madam, your daughter is safely tucked up in bed."

Silly girl. She cannot do anything to my child any more. Of course my child is safe.

"I need some help with my nails, please. Put this bright red colour on them."

I point to the nail varnish and stretch out my fingers and she shakes the bottle of nail varnish and applies a coat to each of my ten nails. I have ten nails on my fingers and thumbs. It is good to have some kind of certainty in one's life. My husband continues to read his Bible while this operation is going on.

"Strange," I say to the room in general, "strange that the President should invite the gentry of this city as well as the diplomatic corps to a party, and stranger still that we should honour his invitation."

"People are strange," says my husband. He is looking at me thoughtfully. Does he think I am strange?

"I remember the hue and cry after the hanging; this country cut off from the international community; the threats. Some said they'd leave Nigeria… and now the President hosts a dinner party and these very people are attending it."

I can see my husband is pleased to find me so consciously lucid.

"Why are *you* going? I thought you wouldn't want to – given your opinion of the President."

"Curiosity," I say, and blow on my nails so that they can dry faster. Nurse, though she has completed her task, is still in the room. Our bedroom. The bed is there where we conceived both children. The carpet which our naked toes touch is beneath our feet and there are the sheets and the pillows on which our bodies toss in fever or lie down in peace and in love.

"You can go now, Nurse. Thank you very much."

"You look lovely, Madam."

"No, I do not."

"Yes you do," says my husband.

The two of them agree that I look lovely. I put on my necklace and earrings. Nurse gasps.

"You may go, Nurse. Wait for us downstairs."

She rises and glides out of the room; we can hear the soft tip-toes of her shoes as she goes down the stairs.

"You didn't have to talk to her that way you know."

"No I didn't."

He continues with his reading. "Ready?"

I do not reply but reach for my shawl and he escorts my bulk to the living room below. Nurse smiles.

"Have a good time!" she cries as we close the door and step into the back of the car which is being driven by Nurse's betrothed. As usual, we are one big happy family. He is chatty. His exuberance is offensive. "I've got something to show you, sir! Maybe when you see it you'll give me a bonus!"

My husband asks him what the something is and he clucks and then he giggles. Our chauffeur clucks and giggles. He will not disclose the something. The drive, mercifully, is continued in silence. I watch the night and the fluorescent glare and the muddled shapes of pedestrians. We stop at a checkpoint. One of the soldiers uses his gun to point at a bag which rests on my husband's lap. My husband has a bag full of leaflets about the outreach mission that is going to be held sometime later this year. He intends to distribute them at the President's party. He wants these people who hang others to know God and become new creatures in Christ. The soldier scrambles through the bag.

"A man of God?"

My husband invites him to the outreach.

"Move on!" shouts the soldier. He has spied an expensive-looking BMW behind us. We move on. The presidential mansion is in full view. It brims with lights. Peacocks strut the lawns as do uniformed soldiers and other officials who come to greet us. It is hard to distinguish between the peacocks, the soldiers and the officials, except that the soldiers are toting guns.

The hall is abuzz with people dressed up in swirls of rich colours. I feel dizzy looking at the scene. Immediately my husband opens his briefcase and, spurning the cocktails, whiskey and so forth, begins to distribute the leaflets about the Christian Outreach. Well, I think, he *is* a man of mission. He has gone on sabbatical leave to organize the Grand Outreach. He wants to save Nigeria, set it free from the likes of Butcher Boy through prayer and God's Word. He's surrendered his Linguistics for the Word. The word and the Word. I admire him. Wish I had his singleness of mind – in spite of the muffled giggles I'm hearing.

The President walks over to us, then pauses and claps my husband on the back. "Leaflets at a dinner party? Religious tracts?"

He is amused and his body, which was pencil-thin when he assumed office but is now a hearty meat-eater's bouncing tub of flesh, shakes with laughter. Relaxation on the faces of those in the hall.

"I, too, am a Man of God! I heard about your incident with the beggars and God advised me to deal with them in no uncertain terms. My babalawos agreed – no important nation should have beggars in its midst. I know you support me – God does not allow dissension… That wretched poet I had to have hanged… Madam, how are you? Three Blind Mice, eh?"

His voice booms. Someone rings a bell. The President is about to make a pronouncement. "So many people have tried to kill me, assassinations, bombs, even poison!"

We wait for the remainder of his utterance. "But I'm still here! This must mean that God is on my side and on the side of this great nation. Oh yes! Even after I authorized the hanging of that rascal poet with his stupidities, his treasonous poetry – which was not that rhyming anyway – people thought I would hang for sure.

Our country was disgraced, they said. They even had the audacity to call me 'Butcher Boy', but look at me tonight! Look at us, the *crème de la crème* of the nation, the diplomatic corps! We are here celebrating military democracy and eating and drinking, eating bits, no, chunks of the national cake which I have baked very well. Cheers! God is on my side!"

My husband's face tightens. I decide to feign discomfort. It is often useful to be a woman in certain circumstances. This is one of those circumstances.

"Aaagh!" I scream. I'm having a wonderful time and I remember that my nails have been painted crimson by Nurse. I slide to the carpeted floor and hold the feet of my husband and wave one hand with its five crimson nails in the air and I scream "Aaagh!" My husband knows I'm play acting, but he is still tense with anger.

I really do not want him to sin. So I do a Mary thing. I lie on the floor and start reciting the nursery rhyme which floods to my head:

Three blind mice
Three blind mice
See how they run
See how they run
They all ran after the farmer's wife
Who cut off their tails with a carving knife
Did you ever see such a thing in your life
As three blind mice?

When we go home... No I do not sleep. I write to learn something about Quamina. I need to know what makes his equivalent in my novel... I need to know what makes Gardener tick. He is in the interior with Mary. Rosita managed to stay behind... developed an illness and couldn't accompany her new mistress... I ask you! So Mary, Mrs. Pearsons, Gruegel and of course the infamous McTurkeyen, who is trying to catch a runaway slave, are all in the interior.

★ ★ ★ ★ ★

Quamina gasped at the length-stretchedness of the land, the openness of the sky. When he had run away that first time he had not known where he was going. He could not remember how far he had gone; he could only remember the thud of his heart as the dogs and the white men closed in. Idly he wondered why McTurkeyen had insisted he be the only slave to... Then the Amerindian settlement came in sight and distracted his thoughts. What he saw made his heart pound. It was the beauty of it which sang in him and he could easily forget Georgetown, the plantations and the buckras.

This landscape languished under a magical spell. He saw huge rocks burgeoning from the earth in a solid mass of copper brown. Some were moulded in the shapes of faces and he searched for his own face, the shape of it. And then... the colours of the sky merged into each other in a musing of bright azure, pale blue and a suffusion of lavender, which shamed his delight with its utter innocence. And then the huts of the Amerindians beneath the mountains of rock: conical-shaped, sloping thatch made from the fibres of a palm which had been knotted and twisted by the deft fingers of the women folk – they were roofs claimed by a comforting silence. It was the silence of the night in the middle of the day and it entered his heart, and he felt, rather than saw, the mountains of sandstone, full-bellied, slope-ambling towards them. There they were, the Cukenam and Roraima mountains seen from the South. Twin mountains. The living rock and the silent patience of earth beneath. The open, smoking fire. The dark forms of the Indians walking in single file as he would have liked to walk. As he would walk. In time.

"Quamina, get some rest, I say." This is Captain McTurkeyen.

★ ★ ★ ★ ★

94

This is scary. Not because Quamina sees freedom in the land of the interior but because of McTurkeyen. I have an uneasy feeling about him and wonder if he's more complicated than I thought. I don't know. God, please, please help me.

That chauffeur-cum-gardener – call him what you will – has a surprise for my husband. What sort of man would be the betrothed of Nurse, anyway? Probably an arranged marriage. It doesn't seem to me that they have anything in common. No doubt Mother of Nurse was behind their union. She, too, is a secretive type. Some church members told me that she was Butcher Boy's wife in the early days when he was a private in the army, but I haven't had the courage to ask her if that's true.

I'm back in hospital. Apparently I became too excited after that party at Butcher Boy's and need to get some rest. This time they've given me a larger room and if I get out of my bed I can look through the windows and see the garden. It's serene; presumably they believe I also shall become serene. Let's hope my family will not come; I mean the extended one with Nurse and her cohorts.

Let's see… I've got C for my children intact and I've got an O for Obscurantize and the next letter in the Hangman's Game is N. Have to think of a good mazy clue that Nurse can't puzzle out…

Perhaps I can get some more writing in before the hospital nurse comes to serve me supper. The telephone is ringing. I thought I was meant to be kept quiet. I pick up the receiver. My husband is on the line. I sense an undercurrent of disturbance. The Outreach not going as planned? He's sorry about telling me off about that shindig at Butcher Boy's mansion? I'm pregnant. I have to take things easy. I shall be self-righteous in a nonchalant way; let him be hurt a little and then I'll relent.

"Yes, I'm very well, thank you." Silence.

"You're sure you're OK? I'm sorry about the other night."

I'm crisp. "I'm very well, thank you."

Silence. It's now time to ask him if he's alright.

"Are you OK yourself?"

"Oh yes. Everything's just fine."

Clearly it isn't; he has that edge to his voice. Time to relent.

"What's the matter?"

His tone echoes relief. Our quarrel is over and he can now go on to other things. "It's the driver…"

"Quamina?"

"Who is Quamina?"

"I'm sorry. You were saying?"

"The driver – Nurse's fiancé?"

"What about him?"

"You remember he said something about a surprise when we were going to the presidential dinner?"

"Indeed I do. What's he up to?"

"He sat me down this morning… Said he had a confession to make."

"And?"

"He used to work for the President and ran away just before he came to our place. He was a kind of personal batsman – I think they call it that – to the President."

"And?"

"He told me of a dreadful happening at the President's mansion. That's the reason he ran away and wore dark glasses when he drove us to the dinner… So he wouldn't be recognized."

"What happened? What did he see or what did he hear? I honestly can't think of anything worse than the hanging of my friend."

"Gardener says he saw the President with a child, a girl whom he himself had procured for the man… The President raped her and Gardener witnessed it."

"So? That surprises you?"

"That's not the worst part. Butcher Boy roughed her up, beat her so badly that she died on the spot. Our gardener was told to bury her as a kind of loyalty test to the President."

"Are you saying what I think you're saying?"

"Yes my dear. I'm afraid we're harbouring a…"

"Does Nurse know about this? Why did he tell you, in any case?"

"I don't know if Nurse knows about it. She probably doesn't. She's a very moral girl…"

"Yes of course she's a very moral girl; anybody with hair like that is bound to have superior moral qualities."

"Don't start!"

"Why do you suppose the driver told you about it? You in particular?"

"As old Hamlet said, 'There's the rub'; he wants to overthrow Butcher Boy's regime and he wants me to assist him."

"You can't be serious?"

"I am… It's so preposterous. His argument is that since I'm a man of God, no one will suspect anything. He wants to use the Outreach as a kind of cover for a revolt to overthrow Butcher Boy's government. He's already been stashing away loads of ammunition. He's already contacted people, men in the East, the North, everywhere…"

"What did you tell him?"

"Of course, I don't agree with everything he said. We want freedom, but freedom will come through God and no one else. Ours is to pray."

"But what did you actually tell Gardener?"

"I told him that as a Man of God I couldn't agree to anything like that… I told him 'No' in no uncertain terms. But he didn't seem to believe me and said he would do his part if I would do mine."

"Darling, don't worry about a thing. I'd like to see both Nurse and her so-called fiancé as soon as you can arrange it."

"Don't discuss this with them. I want your word."

He really does need my word and my words. I shall have to sit up until the wee hours of the morning with Quamina and the rest of them. I say to my husband, "When this is over, you owe me a big thank you." And when I drop the telephone, I'm thinking Quamina/Gardener thoughts.

In my novel *Three Blind Mice*, Quamina wheedles his way into

Reverend Wray's life and then, somehow, gets Smithers to make him Chief Deacon. In that position, he's got immense power, given the numerical strength of the slave population and the fact that hundreds of slaves tramp from plantations like Montrose, La Bonne Intention, Vryheids Lust, and of course his own plantation, Success, to Bethel Chapel. Clearly he plans to use the church as a cover for the revolt. The revolt he'd led some years back had failed for lack of planning; he'd run away and been severely punished. This time giving more thought to the plans.

Strange that the Gardener should have been in the military and a personal aide to Butcher Boy. If he left the President's set-up, that means he's a wanted man. Nurse most likely knows this; she's a knowing sort of girl, that one. But why am I still so uneasy, afraid of what will happen when Jesus says, "Fear Not!"? I won't be afraid again in my life once I've won the game. I won't ever be afraid of anyone or anything. And I won't be afraid of my thoughts.

I should go back to my novel but I don't. Instead I walk to the window and look out at the hospital garden. They've really tamed a wilderness of grass here. There's a rumour going round that the President himself owns this building – as well as the private hospital he has in the grounds of the presidential mansion. That one, I hear, is fully equipped with the latest medical apparatus and the latest drugs. He's even imported a batch of doctors and nurses and heart specialists from Europe and the States as staff. That man will need all the help he can get. Fancy saying that God approves of him because he's managed to escape assassination umpteen times. He thinks he's God, that's the truth of it. He will poison, shoot and hang anyone who threatens his power. But he's hanging himself; he has the rope in his own hands. But why haven't the people revolted yet? I can't understand it. A patient lot. Some of them, anyway. Clearly, Gardener is not.

I look at the lawn and the hibiscus hedge. There are a few frangipani trees in flower, some with cream-coloured petals, some a deep pink on the way to blood red.

"There's a man who says he wants to see you, Madam."

"Might I ask who this man is?"

The nurse gives me the look over and says, "Madam, I think you'd better get into bed."

I am obedient and she tucks me in, pulling the coverlets over my bulging stomach. I allow her to arrange the cushions, the pillows to prop up my back. I have been obedient just so that she, in turn, will be obedient.

"Who is this man? Do I know him?"

"He says he knows you. He says he will only leave the premises if he can see you."

"How does he know me? How does he know I'm here anyway?"

"Perhaps I'd better get him."

"Please do. I had no idea life could be so exciting in this hospital."

She returns with none other than Nurse's fiancé.

"This is an unexpected surprise," I say dryly.

"I had to speak alone to you in private... I spoke to your husband about it... I don't know if he informed you?"

"Does Rosita, I mean, does Nurse know of this visit?"

"Not yet. But she will, she will."

He pulls a chair over to my bed and sits down.

"I was thinking..."

It is reassuring to know that this man has a brain which he can use to think.

"I was thinking that you being pregnant and knowing the President and... I know how you felt when your friend was hanged, I know you will want some sort of revenge..."

Like his wife-to-be, this man knows everything.

"I'm a Christian. I believe that the only way to right the order of things is to hand over everything to God."

When I say this I'm not really sure I believe it. Sometimes I think God needs a nudge, even though, of course, He doesn't. Look what happened when Sarah tried to nudge God. God told Sarah and her husband Abraham that he would give them a child when Sarah was past childbearing age. Years passed. Still no child. So Sarah made Abraham lie with her househelp so they could have the child God promised. The result? Palaver until God took over and gave them the real child He promised them. Anyway, the Gardener... I'm watching his throat; it is round.

"Will you help me?"

"Help you do what?"

"Will you help me get rid of Butcher Boy?"

"I've just told you that I'm handing everything over to God."

"God helps those who help themselves."

"I thought you'd already spoken to my husband."

"He is a man of God. I feel, I feel that…"

"He is a man of God and I am a woman of God."

"Madam, all I ask is for you to think about it. I want to know if you are behind me."

"Behind you?"

"With me."

It might be interesting to consider this man's plan, whatever it is. He can distinguish between the nuances of behind and with. On the other hand… my hand, of course… I tell him that I will think about it. I watch his large head, his dense black skin, his bandy legs. I know his craving for freedom.

"Do you have children?" I query.

He grins. "I have children though I am not yet married to Nurse."

"Are they, are these children yours and Nurse's?"

"Madam! What I will say is that the President … when I left off working for him… my children disappeared."

I have to stall and I say, "I'll get back to you. Next time, perhaps, when you wish to see me you could simply come during visiting hours, as you did before. It's easily arranged." I ring the buzzer and when the nurse escorts him out of the room I call her back and tell her that the visit is to be hushed up. The hospital staff is only too ready to comply with my wishes.

I have to do some more writing, some more playing of the Hangman's Game. I take out my paper with the drawing of the hangman's structure and ponder again the clue for the third letter in the game; this game which I shall win. Think I'll call up Nurse. She sounds nervous when she answers the phone.

"Have you had any thoughts about the letter?"

"The letter, Madam?"

"The letter for the Hangman's Game. You have to think of the third letter."

"Is that how far we've gone?"

100

"We," and I emphasize the "We", "have not gone anywhere. The third letter of the word I'm thinking about. The third letter is what I want you to guess. What is it?"

"What's the clue, Madam?"

"He was spurned and rejected. A man of sorrows. Acquainted with grief."

"That's the clue for the third letter?"

"Yes Nurse, that is the clue for the third letter."

"Madam, are you thinking of Moses in the Bible? M for Moses. He went through much hardship."

"Hardship," I repeat. "No, Nurse. It's not M for Moses; it's N for Nazarene."

I drop the phone and I'm feeling better already and on my drawing I add the body of the man who is being hanged. I've got the head and the neck and the body. I've now got the C and the O and the N parts of my word. Here it is:

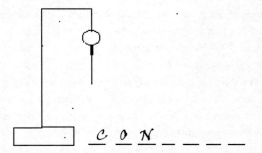

Ouch! CON... con, conniving...

What's John up to in my novel? The runaway slave has been caught by McTurkeyen. Mary and Gruegel and Pearsons are making their way back to Georgetown and from there they'll go to their respective plantations. But what has John been doing with himself? It had better not be a Sarah-nudging-of-God-Abraham thing.

★ ★ ★ ★ ★

John went to his study, an L-shaped room, his desk facing a window. Boxes of books stood waiting to be unpacked. He pulled open a drawer and took out his diary. It was a present from Mary, and she, with the teary knowledge of his mission in the colony and its importance for him had said, "This is for you, my love. You must promise me faithfully to record everything that happens in Demerara." He was overwhelmed by her gesture, but the sadness in her... He dipped a quill pen in an ink pot and began to write.

Arrived after long voyage. Mary unsettled. The Governor a pompous ass and Captain McTurkeyen a man to be watched. Have dispatched Mary to the interior. She'll be away for two to three weeks. I need the time to get organized. Oh this country! The evils of slavery abound everywhere. Even on this plantation; I shall have to have a word with Mr. Hamilblade, the overseer, though I'm uncertain of the outcome of any discussion with that man. Like most of the white buckra, as the slaves call us, he appears dissolute. On our day of arrival we saw a number of slaves being sold into auction. Some were in the stocks. Their punishments far outweigh their crimes. They are treated like beasts of burden, animals. Oh Lord my God, will you not hear the cry of the oppressed? The day after Mary's departure I heard a commotion outside and went to see what was happening. There was a black woman, naked as the day she was born, lying spread out on the ground. She fought with such energy, biting and scratching, that I thought she would overpower those holding her down, but a big burly Negro, stripped to the waist and with the overseer looking on, whipped her severely. She belongs to this plantation and her crime was to feign sickness to prevent field work. She was held down by no less than four men and as the whip fell and cut her back, the blood flowed. Her body writhed after each lash and when they had finished with her she was limp but still screaming the most vitriolic curses that must have ever passed the lips of one of the fairer sex. It appears that whether in slavery or not, the female has the energy to rebel against anything she so wishes. Mary herself is no exception in this. I am distressed by her outbursts of what can only be termed madness. It has been nearly four months since we lost the child and I am sure the good Lord had a plan even in that. I can only surmise that had the child lived it would have interrupted my plans for this mission.

Perhaps Mary will return from the interior of Demerara a new person and will be a proper mate in helping me carry out my duties. One can only pray.

He paused a moment in his writing, looked at the stacks of boxes filled with books – his own private collection and some Bibles and hymnals which the London Missionary Society had given him to distribute to the slaves. Though few of them could read, he would teach them no matter what that upstart of a Governor said; bumbling Murrain would be easy to deal with. Captain McTurkeyen, with his reputation for ruthlessness and as the best slave catcher in the area, might be a different story.

He would have to proceed cautiously to realize his mission, but it was important that the slaves understood the Word of God for themselves. He would be the man to guide them to the greater glory of God.

With a start he remembered the anti-slavery and abolition tracts he had brought from England. Where had he packed them? Which box? Ah yes!

He sighed. He had given them to Mary for safekeeping. He must not fear colonial authority. God was with him. God would guide him. Apart from his constant distress over the manifestations of slavery's evils and that dreadful episode at the Governor's party – and Mary had even had the audacity to return to the mansion against his wishes – apart from that, he was becoming more acclimatized to Demerara. He had met many of the slave congregation who had come to greet the new "Massa Reverend" as they called him. He was impressed by their zeal and especially taken by the enthusiasm of Quamina who, after showing him his carving of a black Jesus Christ, pleaded to be made Deacon of Bethel Chapel. A queer fish that one, but committed to the things of God. He had promised Quamina that services would start on the Sunday after his wife's return from the interior.

Rosita knocked on the study door. "Here is the cough mixture you asked me to bring." She placed a tray with the medicine bottle, a glass and a jug of water on his desk.

"Thank you, but you've forgotten the spoon."

"I'm sorry, Master Reverend Smithers. Please pardon me. I shall go and get it."

He could not concentrate on his work as he waited for her return. *Good person to have around the house.* The Governor's statement niggled him. She looked so pure. Could Mary be right? Mary and her nursery rhymes. She had said that Rosita was nothing but a higgledy-piggledy black hen. She lays eggs for gentlemen.

He did not want the burden of unwanted love. He had put away such foolish things the moment he had entered Silver Street Chapel and God had flowed into his soul. He attempted to read but could not. There was a burning sensation in his chest and throat and he poured himself a glass of water. He drank quickly. Rosita. He should not be attracted to her. He must put his desire for her behind him. He would not follow that path again. He had his mission. He had his wife who, in her contrary way, might yet be an able assistant. He had to get these feelings for Rosita out of his mind. If thy eye offends thee, pluck it out. And thy heart... He needed the spoon for his cough mixture and the girl was taking her time.

He went to the kitchen. She was there reading, sitting on a stool, her back to him. He gazed at the narrow shoulders tapering into a small waist and the folds of material bunched under her seat. He regarded her bent head, its shining black tresses undone. He could feel himself wanting to cough. Desperately he tried to check it and with an effort succeeded.

That unassuming grace. Prayers to ward off the sin he did not want and should not want hung in the silence. Then the cough he could hold in no longer shattered the room. She turned, upsetting the stool, the book, her eyes growing larger. A slow blush crept into her cheeks.

She seized her hair and began to plait it. She reached for a piece of cloth to cover her head; he watched her, feeling a tenseness in his thighs.

She belonged to another man. She was a slave. He should content himself with watching. He should not, as a man of God, succumb to this longing. He had promised himself. He had promised God. And God was watching with his omnipotent eye. Yet why was He granting him this temptation of woman's flesh? To strengthen him against the desire for flesh? Or was she chosen by Satan to tempt him? Was this woman, this girl-woman sent to him to make him fall? Mary's voice mocked him. Higgledy-piggledy, my black hen... No it could not be true of this girl. This cream-coloured rose. He must say something. Say something harsh to her to free himself. But maybe it was God who sent her and not Satan. It was so difficult to discern right from wrong in this slave colony.

"The spoon, Rosita."

She turned her back to him.

"Rosita!"

"Sir?"

"Do not be insolent. You are to call me Reverend Massa Smithers."

"Yes, Reverend Massa Smithers."

"So this is what you do. You read when you are supposed to be working. You forgot to bring me the spoon." He paused. He was beginning to sound like Mary.

"I am sorry. It will not happen again."

As usual, her perfect command of English surprised him into a tenderness that he fought not to reveal. He had to find the handle to drive her out of his mind completely.

"It has come to my attention that you have been given to er... certain acts of immorality with the gentry in the area."

"I do not know what you mean, Reverend Massa Smithers."

"You may call me sir."

"Yes, sir."

He could see a saucepan about to boil over. She followed his eyes and began to walk towards it, a cloth in her hand.

"Leave it. This is a matter of far more importance. I cannot have you living in this house, in a reverend's house... Your reputation is mine."

She ignored him, blew out the fire with lips whose pout pained him, and removed the saucepan. She wiped her hands on her apron.

"I see you are disobedient, too."

"Too?"

"You have been the mistress of several gentry in the area."

"That is not true."

"I have come here to tell you that if it has been your wont to indulge in fornication, adultery... I, the Pastor of Bethel Chapel, cannot allow it."

He waited for her to speak, mesmerized by her grace as she sat in a semblance of composed reading. She had not given him the means to sublimate his longing. He was fascinated by her as never before. He walked to her stool and surprised himself with a swoop of the head and a burning mouth which left a kiss on hers. A kiss on her mouth; an embrace in his arms which encircled her as she claimed his mouth. His mind reeled. He fled the room. If he had looked back he would have seen her bent over, with her head between her legs, clamping her head as if trying to deafen sound.

★ ★ ★ ★ ★

John and Rosita. And Mary. First the corn incident. Now this. Am I simply imagining things? Too many uncertainties; I must keep writing. But what are they doing at home? My daughter must be having her afternoon nap. The chauffeur might be washing down the car or mowing the lawn or clipping the hedges. He could well be clipping the hedges. He has big shears which go snip and grind and crunch in a most delicious way. I have given my character Mary some scissors. She can use them to snip cloth and if she ever takes to gardening she will need even larger scissors. Scissors are useful.

*****

John thinks me mad. He thinks the loss of my sweet rose, my dead baby, has made me mad. I am mad but not with that. I am maddened by seeing the embrace in their avoiding eyes.

Something had to be done. A levelling between herself and the girl-woman. She had seen John looking at her, and John had seen her looking. Rosita. The girl's hair was even longer than hers. She rarely had it loose, preferring to plait it in multiple braids. Her eyes – those beautiful eyes.

"Shall I make the bed, Madam?"

The bed she slept on with John was being touched by Rosita's hands. Her fingers were touching the cloth that covered their bodies.

"Don't! Stop making the bed!"

"Yes, Madam."

"Sit on this."

Rosita sat on the stool facing an oval mirror. It was the first time she had been called to the room. Madam had always insisted on cleaning it herself. It was the smallest bedroom in the house. A double bed, a window with cotton curtains that hung to the floor, and the mirror facing her. It was true what Quamina and the others had said. She *was* strikingly beautiful. Those eyebrows, her large eyes, the lashes thick and long, her red mouth. She looked at her neck, tapering to her narrow shoulders. It was some moments before she realized that Mary was staring at her. Their eyes met in the mirror.

"Have you ever seen yourself before, my dear?"

"I don't understand, Madam."

"Have you ever seen yourself in a mirror?"

"Once or twice, Madam. I have little time for such things."

The black so and so. The nigger child who wanted to dip into the pot of her sweet John hadn't seen herself in a mirror! Only once or twice, indeed! But what did he see when he saw Rosita? Well she would control that seeing.

Once upon a time in a country of forests there was a queen. She knew she was beautiful. The mirror spoke and told her so. It was a man-mirror who knew about women. It should have been a woman-mirror. Women knew about their own beauty. She knew it. Often, after a gathering, John couldn't remember what the women had looked like – who had black hair, who was blonde, whose shoulders sloped. But she, Mary, could remember every hurting physical detail which vied with hers. It was necessary. It was a question of survival. Hers. And his. Together.

The queen asked the man-mirror who was the fairest of them all. He always replied in the same way in a bored tone of voice. The pretence. As if the outward physical flesh wasn't important. The mirror always said that she was the fairest and the queen felt beautiful. The mirror never lied. Then one day the queen addressed the mirror and the mirror told her Snow White was more beautiful than she. She fumed and stamped her pretty feet. Then she decided to act.

How did Rosita come by her complexion? She could pass for white. Not snow white, but definitely white. Her skin was soft and creamy white.

The Queen, in old-crone disguise, gave Snow White a poisoned apple and sweet Snow White sank her teeth into the apple, collapsed and died. Then the queen knew she was again the most beautiful woman in the Kingdom.

"What's your favourite food, Rosita?"

"Madam, do you have a fever? Malaria always catches those who are new to Demerara."

"I do not have malaria. I asked you, what is your favourite food? It's corn isn't it? Don't lie. It's corn. I've seen you heaping your plate with it in the kitchen."

"I like corn, Madam."

"Yes of course you do."

"Will Madam be needing anything more, I…"

"Don't move. I've got something for you. You say you've only seen yourself in a mirror once or twice?"

"Yes, Madam."

"Well have a good look… That's right… You might not see yourself again like this for a very long time."

A poisoned apple. The queen in the story killed Snow White by

109

making her eat a poisoned apple. There are no apples in Demerara. No it couldn't be a fruit. The fruit in Demerara were not English fruit. But she had to do something to stop Rosita's beauty in its tracks, the beauty that John saw but pretended he didn't see. She knew he saw it. It was mirrored in his eyes. He didn't fool her. The dwarfs in the fairy tale – seven of them. That number seven. Seven, a shortened life. Seven days it took to create the world. Only seven. Creation and life. And a dwarfed, belittled, shortened, dwarfed seven: death.

Rosita was killing her life. Rosita already had three children and probably had more in her to come. The dwarfs helped Snow White. Before the queen poisoned her, they helped Snow White to hide in the forest. The queen only found out what was happening when she consulted her mirror. Then she killed Snow White and she was free of her. And then… and then, wouldn't you know? A handsome Prince walks by and sees the dead Snow White lying in a coffin with the poisoned apple in her mouth. The Prince kisses her and with his love Snow White is alive again.

John was her Prince. No one else would have him. Not her John. No one. No situation. No thing.

"Rosita, loosen your hair. Yes… Now brush it. Take my brush, Rosita, and brush your hair."

The girl sat like a statue, her movement frozen.

"Brush it! I said brush it! You're very beautiful aren't you?"

"Madam I don't know, I…"

"You're very beautiful aren't you? Tell me you're very beautiful."

"I am very beautiful."

"Who told you you're very beautiful? Is it the mirror? Is it my husband? Is it John? Tell me, girl."

"It is the mirror, Madam."

It was only then that Rosita noticed the scissors. They were huge cutting scissors made especially for a seamstress. They had big sharpened blades.

"Now take your clothes off."

"Madam is not feeling well. Please let me go and get Madam a drink."

"Going to get me a drink? I'm your mistress. Do as I tell you or I'll have you put in the stocks. It was in the drink you gave my husband that evening at the Governor's house wasn't it? I know about you niggers and your obeah and your potions. You put something in my husband's drink. Auntie Lou helped you. Take off your clothes."

"Please Madam… if I have done anything to offend you…"

"Your body is your offence. Take off everything… Oh dear, oh dear, oh dear, so your hair is nice there too. Turn around and tell me what the mirror says."

"It says I am beautiful, Madam."

"Yes the mirror says you are beautiful. Good arms, a small waist. Turn around. Good buttocks. You would make a good sale. I must talk to the governor about that. He seemed anxious to get rid of you. Or was that Auntie Lou's doing, too?"

"Please Madam. Please let me get dressed."

"You never forget your place. That's a good sign in a slave. Who taught you such good English? For heaven's sake, Rosita stop crying! Who taught you such good English?"

"The… the Reverend Wray, Madam, in secret…"

Mary moved closer to Rosita, still holding the scissors. Then with quiet deliberation she pointed them at Rosita's neck. The girl screamed as the beaks of silver touched her skin, then the blades were opened and were grinding and snipping through the girl's tresses.

Snip. Snip. Snip. The hair, black and long and shining, lay in a heap on the floor.

Rosita opened her eyes.

"Stand up," said Mary, her manner businesslike. "Now," she said, holding the girl by her shoulders. "What does the mirror say? You don't have to ask it anything, of course, but just tell me what the mirror might say."

"Madam, the mirror says I am not beautiful."

"The mirror says you are not beautiful."

The mirror looked at the two women, holding them both in its searching, reflecting gaze. It saw the most beautiful girl it had ever seen with her black hair jagged, standing up as if in a frightened halo. It saw a woman with burnished auburn hair piled on top of her head, her face strained and curiously dead.

"May I get dressed now, Madam?" Her hands flitted to her breasts covering them and then to her pubic hair.

Mary's eyes rested on the hair. She took up the scissors again.

"We're not finished yet."

111

"Please, Madam, I implore you. Please."

The scissors in her hand, Mary noticed a scar traversing the girl's stomach in a long dark line.

"What is that? Have you ever been cut?"

"Yes, Madam. I had to be cut because of the twins."

"You were cut? The twins?"

"Yes, Madam. Auntie Lou, my mother, had to cut me or I would have died."

Mary turned to the window.

"Take your clothes and get out of my bedroom. How many times have I got to tell you never to enter my bedroom? This is our private room. This is our bed. This…"

She looked at the mirror.

"This is my mirror. Get out."

She lay on the bed, clasping the pillow in her arms.

"When you've finished dressing, make me a drink. Coconut water will do. Then you can take me around the slave quarters. What with the heat and the sounds, the journey into the interior… I haven't been able to help John much here. And… Rosita, take those papers. They are in the first drawer… the desk on the right. You'll find papers, speeches… by Wilberforce on the abolition of slavery… Rosita, you are unable to bear your husband any more children are you not?"

★ ★ ★ ★ ★

112

It's so good to be home again; so refreshingly good. I feel as if I have been away from here for weeks on end. Everything is in the mind, I suppose.

My husband is in his study. The door is ajar and I can hear talk: his own rich, deep tones like mahogany wood and the guttural tongue of Gardener. They seem to be engaged in animated conversation. I sit in a chair where I can hear what's going on. This is not eavesdropping, I convince myself. I'm actually trying to save the nation in my own way. My husband sounds grave.

"If I were you, I would desist from such talk. It will only get us into trouble."

Then it is the other voice. "I thought you were a man of God."

"I believe that this should conclude our discussion. I want no more talk like this in my house."

I have to try and piece this brief dialogue together. My husband has told me to mind my own business and not to have anything to do with Gardener's coup propositions. But… Gardener walks past me and nods. He goes outside and soon I hear the sound of the lawnmower scraping away at the grass which does not need cutting. No matter; it keeps him busy. The door of the study is open. My husband does not know I am here. He thinks I'm upstairs in my bedroom writing. And that's where I should be and that's what I should be doing – writing.

He senses my presence.

"Why sweetie, I didn't know you were down here. Writer's block?"

"I never get writer's block. I have enough words in me to last several lifetimes."

His tone becomes bantering. "Thankfully we only have one lifetime to concern ourselves with."

"We have two lifetimes," I tell him.

I'm trying to determine whether I should ask him about Gardener's visit. I decide to be patient and wait for him to tell me. After all, he rang me up at the hospital concerning this fellow.

He says, "I do wish you'd rest… I know, let's have some corn."

Immediately I pull my hand away from his. "I, I hadn't realized that this was corn season."

"You've been away, probably slipped your mind."

But my mind is not slipping. If I hadn't been in hospital, I would have known that it was indeed corn season. At such times you can see men and women at junctions, lining the streets, selling corncobs to passers-by. The corn is braised barbecue style, or boiled in large enamel pots and given to you steaming hot, wrapped up in newspaper.

"Does the fact that I've asked you if you wish to have some corn require such deep thought?"

"Yes," I say.

"I'm going to have some corn. Nurse bought it."

"I don't like corn."

"And you don't like Demerara sugar. I like corn. It's not as if I'm asking you to eat it on my behalf, is it?"

"I'd rather you didn't."

"Didn't what? Nurse! Bring that corn, will you?"

I am, it appears, not the only one who listens at doors. The little wretch enters the room with two dishes. One has on it two corn cobs, which offend my eyes, and the other has square coconut pieces. She is so very neat, this Nurse.

"I brought coconut to go with it, Sir. Will Madam have some corn?"

"Madam…" I space out the words "will… not."

She makes to leave but I stop her. "Changed your hairstyle again, I see?"

She has her hair in a Swiss roll. It looks elegant and suits her small flower face. My husband is munching as if his life depends on it. It does.

"Your hair has been getting into the food. I suggest you wear a scarf, no, a hairnet over it; tie it in string – anything. You might even want to have it cut. I think a close-cropped style would do very well! Or you could shave it off."

My husband enters the dialogue and says, "Sweetie, you can't dictate her hairstyle."

"And why not? People, employers do it frequently. Only the other day I was reading that a woman was suspended from her office job because she had her hair done in dreadlocks."

"That's entirely different," he says. "Nurse is one of the family."

Silently I curse. Then I remember that I shouldn't curse and I decide to take a turn in the garden. I walk through the front doors telling them I shall be outside until my daughter arrives from nursery school. But she is already here, running to meet me.

"Mummy! Mummy!" she almost topples me over and the chatter flows. They played with blocks and did finger painting. She proudly shows me a small hand stained with paints.

"You'll have to get washed up. Nurse will help you. I just want to take a stroll in the garden."

She refuses to go in until she tells me every single detail of her morning at school. Teacher read them a fairy story. But it's not the story I had thought. It is "Jack and the Beanstalk". She tells me the story. She is particularly impressed with the giant and asks me if giants still live today and if the President, who appears in one guise or another on TV and on posters in schools and in offices and in supermarkets, is a giant. She has only seen him waist up but wonders if he is as tall as a giant.

"I expect he's a dwarf on the quiet," I mutter, but she insists on asking whether the President is a giant; Mummy and Daddy have met him and have been to a special party at the President's house and she was too small to go and Mummy and Daddy know the President.

"He is a tall man," I say.

"But mummy is he a giant?"

"He's very tall, but I hear he wears platform shoes."

"What are platform shoes, Mummy?"

"They're shoes with blocks in them, a bit like the blocks you played with at school. When you put them into ordinary shoes they become higher and the person who wears them automatically becomes taller and taller."

I rise on my sandalled feet and she giggles. But I'm not let off the hook that easily.

"Daddy doesn't wear platform shoes."

"No he doesn't. He has no need of them. His spirit is so tall. He is a giant among dwarfs."

Unfortunately the word "dwarf" triggers another memory in her. I guess what is coming. The teacher at her school has also recounted the story of "Snow White and the Seven Dwarfs". But before she can begin to retell it, I shoo her into the house. I have my own mission to attend to. The grass of the lawn is now scraped clean like a shaven head. I need to speak to the gardener, though I do not wish to talk of the roses, the bougainvillea, the potted cacti. At the very least, two requests, two deals, two bargains have to be contracted between us. Is he trying to avoid me? I don't think so. He has met a closed door with my husband. I am sure they spoke of a coup. I do not know why he should want my help. There's nothing I can do to help – really help – except pray for this our beloved country. One of the Baptist Churches had its congregation fasting for a hundred days to uphold the nation in this terrible time of need. Right now my mind is focused on a much more profound matter. Namely Snow White and the Seven Dwarfs. The corn issue has already been blotted out. No more corn shall be served in my house, in whatever form, whether boiled or braised in a pot over coal, canned or even raw and ready to be peeled by a saucy maid.

I look around for Nurse's fiancé; he's probably in the small flat at the bottom of our garden, now that he's chopped off the heads of the flowers. He doesn't seem to care much for the roots dimension. And as for his driving skills… Let's just say I don't like his type of fuel, petrol shortage or not. I walk through a tiny gateway at the end of our garden and knock on his door. Sure enough, he is there.

The room is sparsely furnished. Big wooden crates stacked everywhere. His only extravagance is a small TV which has pride of place on a small table, the top covered by vinyl, a snaky, shiny red. The walls are plastered with huge posters which have seen better days. They curl at their grimy edges. There's Nelson Mandela, Che Guevara and Fidel Castro; an old print of a top-hatted stern-faced President Lincoln and another of Nixon. It's been some time since I've been to this flat. I sit myself down on the only available sitting space in the room – his bed. Without the customary greetings usually employed in this country before one gets down to business – just as he acted when he came to see me in the hospital – I ask peremptorily, "Why Nixon?" He follows my stare. He does not seem surprised to see me. "Why Nixon?" I repeat.

"I could say that I just happened to find that poster. But you're an intelligent, perceptive woman. You wouldn't believe me."

"Quite so. I wouldn't."

"I admire his craft."

"You admire a man who sold out his country. This is interesting."

"I admire his cunning. Why did you come to see me? Did your husband tell you of the conversation we had this morning?"

"We'll leave that for later. I prefer to hear from him first hand before I hear from you."

"Fair enough."

"I'm glad you agree. I have a proposition for you."

His eyes light up. I see a soldier's boot on a shelf behind him. I point to it. His face becomes intense.

"The boot belongs to the President."

"You stole his boot? One boot? Why not the whole pair?"

"Only one was necessary. It is a reminder of, of…"

Casually I rise, holding my stomach to protect it, guarding it from what it might see. I want to ascertain whether the President uses blocks in his shoes. He does. The Giant uses platform shoes. I'm grinning.

Gardener is irritated. "This is no laughing matter, Madam. Thousands of our citizens have lost their lives since Butcher Boy came to power."

I remembered the day well enough. I woke up, turned on the radio and heard military music. The music was the same on every station. It was the signal of a military coup. Another one. They had become habitual, a part of life, along with the promises of speedy returns to democracy. Later, it was the face of a then young Butcher Boy and his steady contempt, assuring the nation that the past evils of military government were at an end. The coup, his coup, had been a pushover. He had most of the military elite in

117

the bag. Those who opposed him, or whom he suspected of opposing him in the future, were invited to an important cabinet meeting. We soon discovered why it was important. He had to get on with the democratization process. Namely shooting the opposition dead. That had all happened a while back.

Nixon was grinning and it was time I got back to the house before they came searching for yours truly.

"I'll agree to help you in any way I can, if you get your fiancée to cut her hair. Shave it off."

"But," he stutters, "hair is a woman's pride and glory."

"The Masai think differently."

"Why?"

"Call it a whim of a pregnant woman on the edge. Before I proceed on any deal with you, Nurse has to cut her hair."

"She'll refuse. What'll her mother say?"

"Frankly that's up to you to handle. It's essential to my life, to my emotional well-being... actually it's spiritual... You are more or less married to her. Tell her she's got lice... anything."

He scratches his head. He is no doubt thinking that I'm really on the edge.

"I'll do my best," he says and I take a last look at his room and Butcher Boy's boot and I begin to understand why he wants to rid this country of the President. As for my part of the bargain, which he has not yet spelt out, I am not worried. I walk back to the house and, closing the front doors behind me, shout for Nurse. She approaches with a finger to her pretty lips. I see she is wearing a nice shade of lipstick. She whispers that my daughter is asleep, taking her afternoon nap. My husband has gone to the church. Nurse and I are alone. Anything could happen. I take a long look at her head, which I have no doubt whatsoever will soon be quite shaved. I almost begin to like her and I tell her to go and get some rest.

When she leaves I'm thinking, thinking... That Gardener, he's a dangerous man. I have a feeling that he's not necessarily going to rely on me. On my help. Why should he? The Outreach is scheduled for next week, Sunday. The seventh day. Will he wait that long to start the coup and get things going? I know the meaning of those crates in his flat. I'm almost certain they're crammed with ammunition. He's not an ex-soldier for nothing. He's bound to have contacts – men who are as disgruntled with the regime as he is, or more. So many soldiers in Butcher Boy's army hate their president's guts. They're just waiting for the right time to strike and timing is everything.

That's what I'll do. I'll collapse time and go straight to Demerara 1823 in my novel: the year of the slave insurrection. And I'm going to turn the seven of my hangman's scaffolding the right way round and make it a positive creation seven and not a destructive seven like the seven of revolt. I do not want Nigeria to have yet another coup. We've got to get our freedom alright, but the kind of freedom which will last. I have no wish to be ruled by the likes of Gardener and his hate.

I'm going to look over my notes for Part Two of *Three Blind Mice*... Let's see...

In Demerara, a large group of slave women led by Auntie Lou plan to spearhead a revolt in conjunction with the male slaves. Mary's Salvation Sewing Group has been used as a cover for their meetings. Mary herself has been working hard, if you could call it that, pretending to go evangelizing on various plantations even as far as the East Coast, whereas she is actually updating the slaves on developments for the revolt. It is a process which has taken years and with John's constant criticism of her efforts with the slaves as being "minimal", she has cut herself off from her buckra friends and channels all her energy into planning the revolt, feeling that when it does finally occur, John will see her worth. She will not be his appendage, the missionary's wife, but a woman in her own right who can change the course of history and help to alleviate, if not finally put an end to the institution of slavery.

The many rumours which abound in the colony that the manumission process has already begun make her more determined to liberate the slaves. She does, occasionally, feel some remorse over her stance in relation to John, but reasons that for his own safety it is better if he remains ignorant of the coming revolt. As for John himself, he seems to be completely unaware of what is happening under his very nose. He continues to preach, saying that the slaves are "his slaves" and they would never rebel against the buckras for he has put the fear of God into them

119

through the preaching of many sermons since his arrival in the colony. He says the slaves trust him and he trusts them and he gives Quamina, his Chief Deacon, more and more responsibilities in Bethel Chapel. John even goes so far as to preach from the Book of Exodus in the Bible – the story which narrates the deliverance of the Israelites from slavery – on a day which later turns out to be the eve of the Demerara slave revolt. Indeed, he is so caught up in his own zealous mission that he is blind to the machinations of Quamina, Mary, everyone.

As for Rosita, she yearns to warn John that there is trouble afoot but abandons the idea because she feels guilty for loving him and does not want her personal allegiance to him to mar the outcome of what she perceives to be a higher good: freedom for the slaves. She has distanced herself from John who believes she does not wish to tempt him further. Thankful, he leaves her alone and buries himself in work, consumed as he is by his vision: flaunting colonial authority – particularly in the person of Captain McTurkeyen, teaching the slaves to read and write, declaring that Sunday should be a day of rest and the slaves should go to church regardless of whether they are needed for work on the plantations.

Now Auntie Lou and the Governor… When it is learnt that King George of England has sent directives to begin the manumission process, and that as a first step female slaves are no longer to be flogged, Auntie Lou challenges the Governor concerning the truth of this news. He deems her impertinent and Auntie Lou, distraught, but not too surprised by what she conceives to be a breach in their relationship, deliberately breaks his beloved chamber pot. The Governor summons his overseers and has her whipped with the cat-o-nine tails. She determines to kill him.

For both these long-term and immediate reasons, the women decide that the time for revolt has come. With Auntie Lou as their leader, they join forces with Quamina and the men. The latter, though, refusing to be engaged in what he refers to as a "kitchen war", one in which "a mad white woman" plays an instrumental part, has already been making his own plans with the slaves on the plantations and in Georgetown and on the East Coast regarding the timing of the revolt, a timing which is at odds with that proposed by the women. The women believe that the revolt should take place on the day of the Governor's annual birthday party. Unknown to them, however, Quamina arranges with his men that the revolt should occur a day earlier, on a Sunday, reasoning that the white buckra will be at their church and therefore can be attacked with relative ease. He realizes that he might be missed by John and the absence of the male slaves will be evident in Bethel Chapel. He therefore gives a note to John on the eve of the revolt to "cover" himself. In the end, John is implicated in the revolt by this very note – but that comes later.

The revolt occurs next. The revolt, of course, is represented by the line of the nursery rhyme which reads "She cut off their tails with a carving knife." (I use "tails" to represent certain male appendages which we shall not go into here, as well as tales – the stories of their lives.) The men orchestrate their own demise by pursuing freedom – the farmer's wife – in a perverted, self-seeking way. As for the carving knife, since the farmer's wife used it to cut off the tails of the three blind mice instead of for carving meat, I think it would be fair to say that the carving knife connotes a kind of domestic, personal savagery. All this is in keeping with the network of relationships between the men and the women in the novel, where I see quite a bit of the carving knife device at work …

The revolt. Along with other male slaves, Quamina gets things going by burning down buildings in Georgetown. Anxiously, he awaits the arrival of the slaves from the East Coast, as planned. But the men will never get there. The men will never arrive. Why? Because the Governor suspects that Auntie Lou must have heard him discussing the abolition of slavery directive with his officers and – this is the biggie – knows of his stifling of the Royal Decree commanding that as Governor he must start the manumission process. He has had Auntie Lou whipped and can't rely on her discretion – well, he is not about to take any chances with the possibility of slave rebellion if the slaves got wind of this intelligence so he sends some troops to the East Coast who promptly stockade hundreds of the slaves. He is very much aware that in the history of the colony the worst slave revolt emanated from that area. The Governor then gives instructions for the militia to be brought in to Georgetown on the very day that Quamina decides to "seize the time".

★ ★ ★ ★ ★

Quamina licked his lips. He had managed to get information to the male slaves in Georgetown concerning the new date of the revolt and also to the key plantations. The coachman from the East Coast laughed out loud when he told him that this was not to be a kitchen war conducted by women. It was true that Auntie Lou could hold her own, but Rosita? His face split in a grin. And as for Mary... Mistress Mary...

He stood behind a house on the main road watching the carriages as they made their buckra-filled way to church. Soon they would be singing and listening to their own Word of a white God with their white ears. He had told one of the servers to inform John Smithers that he was sick. Truth was he had always been sick. Bethel Chapel would be crowded with women only, but by the time Smithers suspected anything it would be too late. Another hour for the buckra to settle down and Bristol would blow the horn. He waited restlessly. Freedom was at best an hour away. He swigged from a bottle of rum that Gingo had filched from his master and threw the remainder of the liquid onto the grass.

He squatted on his haunches, once again rehearsing the plan in his mind, which he had called "Deliverance". Today he was an Israelite and Egypt would be left behind for ever.

The gallop of a horse's hooves. He hid behind the building. It was Hamilblade, the overseer from Le Resouvenir plantation. Quamina recognized the dappled flanks of the mare and the brown jacket the man reserved for Sunday service. But what was he doing here in Georgetown? The hour must be nearly up. He listened for the horn. It would be blown thrice and its sound would proclaim death to those who had oppressed him and his. Fleetingly he thought of his children. He had to see them. To get a pass to the plantation to which they had been sent had been impossible, especially after... He grinned. No running away now. Not any more. He was a man and he would fight.

The sound came and he started. He had been waiting, expectant, but had not thought it would materialize so soon. He began to wish he had not thrown away the bottle of rum. He picked up a stick with a piece of cloth wound round it, doused it with oil, lit it and set fire to the building. It caught immediately and the bright flames ran through the wood, licking it with a heady wildness.

He ran, his body crouched, to the stables, to the next house, setting fire to them. A dense cloud of smoke appeared on the horizon. Georgetown had begun to burn. Most of the buckras would be in the church. He hesitated. He could not bring himself to burn the church, St. George's. Already, confused, alarmed faces were flying helter-skelter onto the street. But where were the men from the East Coast? He spotted Hamilblade bearing down on him. He dropped his torch and faced the horse's hooves and slashed at the animal with his machete. The horse reared in pain, causing Hamilblade to fall to the ground. Quamina struck him on his shoulder and ran onto the street. The slaves were shooting at any buckras they saw. Those who did not have muskets used cutlasses, machetes. He passed a dead man, his face wracked with his last pain. He stumbled over another. Where were those men from the East Coast? The buildings were burning and that divided the attention of the buckras from the fighting, but it could not last. He knew his men didn't have enough ammunition. Had his plan failed? Militiamen on horses in their peaked top hats were everywhere. Shooting. Where had they come from? They swarmed the street, some riding ahead of the white ladies in their carriages making for the boats on the river.

He turned around just in time to see a white youth drawing his sword. He threw his machete, aiming at the man's chest and the youth fell with the blade still in him. He cried for mercy and Quamina extracted his weapon and stood watching the blood spread over the man's shirt.

Everywhere the fighting was intense. The buckras had muskets, so many muskets. Without ammunition, some slaves had resorted to throwing stones and Quamina saw them being cut down by musket fire. More militia men. More buckras packing their women and children into carriages and slapping the animals to urge on speed as they headed for the ships on the Demerara River. But for his kind the Demerara River would not part like the Red Sea and make a path for freedom as it did for the Biblical Israelites of old. He came upon the body of a black woman in whose back was a large hole. He turned her over with his foot. He spotted Gruegel and ran towards him. Gruegel's sword was locked with a slave's. He took aim. Hurled his machete at Gruegel's back, watched him topple, die.

Smoke, grey, thick and vaporous, hung over the streets. His throat was parched, his tongue dry. There was a burning sensation in his leg and he knew that he had to run. Hamilblade had seen him. He would be identified. The slaves from the East Coast had not arrived and in the recriminations that would certainly follow this revolt his name would be called. He thought of the meetings night after night with the men; the circles of men around him (like mice, Auntie Lou had said). She had dreamt it: the long years of waiting until he could wait no longer; his deaconship and his teaching of the word of God; the stockpiling of weapons; the plan to burn down Georgetown and each and every plantation in a freedom of fires; burning down the Governor's mansion, McTurkeyen's plantation – McTurkeyen killed. But now, would he ever see his children and see himself for what he really was? The plan had gone awry and he, Quamina, was to blame.

His head was a furnace of throbbing pain and the sound of drums exploding. His legs waddled as he ducked behind houses, behind carts. He would have to run out of Georgetown, but run where? How far could he run? He, Quamina, run? Running and running…

★ ★ ★ ★ ★

Something tells me to call Nurse.

"I want you to get your mother here right now. Here's the taxi fare. And before you go, tell your fiancé that I want to see him, too, OK?"

"Yes, Madam."

"And another thing! We have to meet… I want us to have a meeting before six. My husband will be back by then. There are some things I want to discuss with you. Important stuff. Not a word to anyone. While you're gone you can be thinking of the next letter in the Hangman's Game. The clue is 'the sweet tree of hanging'."

"The sweet tree? More hanging? Madam, is there any hope of me getting one letter of the word?"

"Why are you wearing a scarf on your head?"

She sucks her teeth and walks out of the room and I'm thinking that were it not for the urgency of the time I'd just sack her outright.

I decide to get dressed for the meeting and I brush my hair till it gleams and I tie it in a chignon at the nape of my neck. My husband likes my hair, its blackness, its silky sheen and I think with gratitude of my hormones, which have given it even more of a sheen since the onset of my pregnancy. Nurse, at least, has the good sense to cover her head. Maybe Gardener has already told her of my wishes. She appears again, a smile on her pretty face.

"I thought I told you to go and get… What, what is that in your hand? What are you doing with my scissors?"

"Scissors are very useful, Madam, are they not?"

She moves closer. The bright silver beaks of the scissors are pointing at my unborn child.

126

"Do you really think I am one of the characters in your book, Madam? Did you really believe that you can continue to terrorize me? You piece of shit. I know other words for shit, Madam, which I'm sure you'll be interested in. There's turd for instance… turd and excrement…."

"Get out of this house now, Nurse! Get out of my life!"

The beaks of the scissors are pressing into my stomach.

"Ever since I came into this house – and you call yourself a Christian – you've made my life hell. Sheer hell. 'Nurse, pack my bags! Nurse, fetch my nail varnish! Nurse, Nurse Nurse! Have you got the clue in the Hangman's Game, Nurse? You'd better get the word I'm thinking about, Nurse, or you'll have to go.' Then you tell my fiancé that my hair should be cut."

She drops the scissors on the floor. She removes the scarf and I see her shaved head.

"He shaved it himself, Madam. He said you told him to… you, you!"

"I said get out of this house. Get out of my house!"

"Your house?" she mocks. She bends down and picks up the scissors, pushes the beaks of the scissors further into my stomach. I am so frightened I cannot speak. I cannot even pretend courage when I see the malice in her eyes.

"It isn't a game when the shoe is placed on the other foot is it, Madam?"

"Shoe?" I repeat stupidly.

"Were it not for Master, I'd push these scissors right through you. You and your wretched baby."

She's opening the beaks of the scissors and they grate and squeak in her hands. She throws them on one of the chairs. We're both looking at them. The scissors like a carving knife on the chair. Nurse tells me to sit down. She has been reading my novel, *Three Blind Mice*.

"For your information, Madam, I am not in love with your husband and never have been. Never. Do you understand that? Or do you need another word for that too? Do you comprehend? I do not love your husband – or any other man, for the record. Men! Butcher Boy, my father – a man who has never acknowledged my existence… If it hadn't been for my mother… OK, she did arrange for me to marry 'Gardener'... said I needed *to be protected*... but where has that left me?"

Auntie Lou and the Governor. Deaconess and the President. So she has been married to Butcher Boy all along and this offspring of theirs is in my house.

Nurse stands up on her tiptoes and towers over me.

"No more playing of the Hangman's Game with me. No more meeting. I'm not going to get 'Gardener' or my mother or anyone. Don't try to interrupt. I shall have my say, you stupid piece of shit!"

I'm cowering under this onslaught. I don't know what to say or do.

She glares at me. On her face and in her eyes – malice, then pity, then resignation. "Gardener, as you call him, the man who cared nothing for me..."

"Cared?"

"He's been shot." She says these words without a grain of emotion. As if she was saying a nursery rhyme, without portent, without meaning.

"Yes, Madam. You should have known that, shouldn't you? He's been shot along with hundreds of men on Lekki Beach. He..."

It is only now that her composure leaves her and her body is a silent shudder of weeping.

"Nurse... forgive me. I am so sorry for everything... I... Perhaps blowing your nose would, would, help... I..."

She begins to laugh when I say that. Laughs and laughs and to stop her I have to slap her hard on the cheek – though I'm not sure whether I'm slapping her to bring her to her senses or whether I simply want an excuse to slap her. This woman-child has caused me and mine so much pain. She stays my hand.

"There's no point in holding a meeting. You wanted to plan how we would use the Christian Outreach to overthrow the government... That's why you wanted my mother and Gardener here, wasn't it?"

I nod assent. What else is there to do? I hadn't bargained on this development. Hadn't bargained on this outburst at all. Her Demerara replica, Rosita, wouldn't have...

"We don't have to meet to discuss anything. At the President's dinner party this Saturday my mother will set this country to rights. She has powers."

"You said that you don't love my husband…?"

"It's in your head, Madam! And what if I did? He only has eyes for you. Can't you see that? Are you so blind? For your information, Madam, I am not a character in your book."

"Can you… can you please forgive me… I …"

Nurse has stopped crying. She appears to have the control I crave and she tells me to wait for the President's dinner party and see her mother, Deaconess, set this country aright. Nigeria will be put out of its misery on that day. We shall be free. Her mother, Deaconess, will save the nation. Then for someone who knows of murder past and to come, she transforms remarkably into the proverbial cheeky maid. Advises me, Madam, to finish my novel.

"Hello, you two."

My husband. Hadn't heard him coming up the stairs.

Nurse smiles at him, says, "Good afternoon, sir." Turns and smiles at me with the same smile she smiled at him. Says, "Madam, thank you very much for letting me have the afternoon off." Sallies out of the bedroom on her tiptoes, her feet suddenly looking to me like hooves.

"Sweetie, you're shaking? What's up?"

"I'm OK."

"The President is having another of his dinner parties and you'll never guess what."

"What?" I ask, trying hard to steady my voice.

"The party is being held to promote our Outreach. It's a coup!" he laughs, sitting down in an armchair. "A spiritual coup! Gardener has agreed that this country can only be saved through our prayers and he has somehow managed to connect with some of the President's PR men and they have persuaded the President to host this dinner for that reason. God really does work in mysterious ways. Darling, are you sure you're alright?"

He looks at his watch. "Ah! Good timing! The dinner is going to be announced on the radio. Gardener said…"

"Gardener said?"

We listen to Butcher Boy's announcement. He has been

divinely appointed to rule this great nation of Nigeria. God has advised him to relinquish his powers by the year two thousand and forty. This means that he has a good forty years in store. He will be in his late nineties and a grand old man. He will, he says, as an act of good faith, and to show the nation that his intentions are serious, begin by creating a ministry with the express intention of looking after women's affairs. Women are the underdogs of society and he will start the militarized democratic process by freeing them. Henceforth women are no longer to be battered, either in mind or in body. He will use his wives, or most of them, to effect his plans, especially his long-lost love and former wife, Deaconess. A dinner party will be held at the weekend when he, the President, will speak further to the elite of the nation.

"I thought you'd be pleased," says my husband. "Nigeria will be free. Isn't that what you want? No, don't look at that novel… You're acting strangely…"

"I, I'm not sure I want to go to that dinner. Shit! I…"

Now I don't know whether Gardener was shot or not. That little wretch of a Nurse, whom Mary should have poisoned when she had the chance – and did I write about another dinner at the Governor's mansion? I knew I had meant to at one point, to show how blind the plantocracy were to the plight of the slaves; discussing the news of manumission while they were served by those very slaves.

"Darling I've never heard you say that word before!"

"What word?"

"You said 'shit'. Are you sure you're feeling alright?"

★ ★ ★ ★ ★

I go to say goodnight to our daughter before we go to the President's dinner party.

She is already asleep. Oh if only life were a string of moments like this. I'd take the special jewels of these moments and string them together on a cord, a three-fold cord. This moment sees her little face on a pillow and in the crook of her arm is her teddy bear and at the bottom of the bed is the inevitable book of nursery rhymes. We stand before her, my husband and I, holding hands.

Then we're out of her bedroom and down the stairs. Nurse is half asleep in the living room. I am not half asleep. My mind is running back to the novel. I have this desperate urge to pull up her wrapper and look at her stomach and see if she's been cut by the midwife's knife. But I have to resist the urge. I have to think of some permanent way of getting rid of that girl.

But for now, dinner at Butcher Boy's. I think that I did intend to write about a dinner at the Governor's mansion before the revolt took place, so that I could establish the political climate and simultaneously detail the cruelties of slavery – the many punishments inflicted on the slaves for minor offences and just because they were slaves – the metal mask clamped on the head to prevent the offender from eating and drinking for several days, children sold and their parents never seeing them again.

"What are you doing my dear? What are you writing?"

I don't show him a piece of paper which says: IF I HAVE WRITTEN ANYTHING ABOUT THE GOVERNOR BEING MURDERED AT DINNER, I HEREBY EXPUNGE IT.

We leave the house for the presidential mansion. Butcher Boy is anxious to befriend the Christian Community. As well as fraternizing with babalawos, he wants to align himself with the Christians, just in case things don't work out for him in the babalawo realm.

I wonder how it will all end. May God's will be done. It is not easy living in a country where you can wake up in the morning only to discover that a new president has installed himself. Butcher Boy has remained in power for years. Before, we'd had thirty coups in as many years.

"Where is Gardener?" my husband asks, "I haven't seen him around."

I say nothing as he helps me into the car and takes the wheel. Except for the Nurse incident I feel relatively OK, knowing that nothing untoward will happen. I've taken care of that.

This city at night is a myriad of flickering shadows, dim lamps lighting the tables where vendors sell spirits and food to passersby. The night seems to be quite without stars. We pass various checkpoints, which increase in number and intensity as the

President's mansion approaches; its gigantic gates electrified; its soldiers sauntering, their guns bristling across their shoulders. We are ushered in after presenting the invitation card. In the enormous hall with its Italian marbled floor, purring air conditioners and portraits of His Excellency Butcher Boy on every available space, there are people standing about in knots, most of them fondling cocktail glasses. A steward asks me if I would like some wine. A drop or two will not hurt my baby and I accept. I tell the steward yes, I would like some wine and he asks me if I want red or white wine. I say I would like red wine and he says he's sorry but there's no red wine. While I ponder on this peculiar litany, which he repeats to various people, I am looking around the crowd to see if Deaconess is here. She is. The woman is remarkable. She's dressed to the nines in a very ornate wrapper. She is speaking volubly. I decide to give her a wide berth. I am grateful that I do not have to spend the remainder of the evening worrying that she will poison the Governor, I mean the President. If she only knew what I know she would not be so bubbly.

We are called in to dinner and seated at the many round tables with our names on place-cards. Fake lilies have been flown in from Paris for the ladies. The President has invited us to share in the joy of a new democratic, militarized government that will last until he arrives at a ripe old age. He is hearty as only a man who has made such a decision is hearty. Before dinner is served he makes a speech. He is wearing sunglasses and you cannot see his eyes.

"Fellow Nigerians, I am truly honoured by your presence tonight. This is indeed an auspicious occasion. I have decided, with the divine power given to me, as was customary with the royalty, the kings and queens of Europe, to extend my reign until I reach the year, the age…" A pause for our clapping. The President continues. "As you might have heard on the radio and TV… I have created a ministry especially devoted to women's issues. The women in this country have been bedevilled by very hard circumstances. Child brides, the marriage of child brides in the country, has been stopped. It is now illegal for any man to engage in, in… in child brideship."

I try to catch the eye of my husband who is facing me but sitting at another table. He seems to be engrossed in the President's speech. Do we, does he dare to be otherwise? The President's henchmen are around us; some are dressed in ornate agbadas and expensive suits like the dinner guests. Others wear green suits, white shirts and green ties, the country's national colours. They are, in the tradition of American gangster films, also wearing sunglasses. They are not the same type as the sunglasses worn by the three blind mice in my daughter's nursery rhyme book. Their sunglasses are expensive-looking and glint with a blue shine.

The President goes on to detail the numerous atrocities – his word not mine – committed against women in this country. He has numerous wives. Two of them are in this very dining room. No, three, even if you don't count Deaconess. His wives look at him. I don't believe it… He is beckoning to Deaconess and her black statuesque form walks at this command. Her headdress collides with his sunglasses, causing them to fall off. They embrace; he hastily replaces his sunglasses. He holds her hand.

"Ladies and gentlemen, members of the diplomatic corps, you might not be aware of this, but this woman is also my wife. We have been estranged for many years until recently. This woman…" the President looks Deaconess up and down, from head to toe approvingly, "This woman I present to you as an article of my good faith. She is a nurse by profession, a midwife, and has made tremendous inroads into the medical sciences in this country."

I blink. I didn't know our Deaconess was such an expert.

"And I do not speak of medical science in a Western sense either." He shakes his head from side to side. It is a very large head with a cherubic face attached to it, which makes him all the more sinister.

"Oh no! Deaconess is skilled in native medicine. Pick up any herb, any grass from the earth of our beloved country and she can tell you its uses. She is, my dear friends, a wonderful woman. A woman to be lauded, praised, exalted, verified. Her powers are such, my dear guests, that she has even been known to sit in her room and with her mind take off the skin of someone who has treated her cruelly. Oh yes! Don't be fooled by these pretty dimples!"

There is a murmur among the guests. Deaconess whispers something in his ear.

"The good lady does not wish me to talk about this aspect of her powers. But I shall. It is only fitting that I do so. I visited the man in question when his skin was removed and it was not a charming sight."

I begin to picture a man without skin.

"Indeed, my honoured guests, Deaconess is a strong Christian leader."

A pause for applause. It comes. It has been recorded earlier. The President calls these tapes booster applause tapes. He likes to be sure about the outcome of everything, especially applause.

"And that is why, and it is for these variety of reasons, I now pronounce her Minister of Women's Affairs for the new ministry which I have founded."

On cue, the applause. Unfortunately, NEPA, the National Electric Power Authority, is having a bad night and so the pre-recorded applause doesn't come this time round. All we can hear is a spatter of flesh on palm.

Deaconess is led away. I wonder if it is to the kitchen to prepare some poison in the dark. I've scotched that snake. But have I word-killed it? I sense her trying to catch my eye but I do not dare to look. Be anxious for nothing. The President comes to the end of his speech. I hear the words of it with my heart.

"… Outreach in which many souls will be won for Christ. Invitations have already been sent out to every single part of this country by telephone, by letter, by fax machine, by ESP."

He is beaming loudly. He has omitted thuggery. The thuggery machine of his soldiers who will force everyone to attend. I dare not look at my husband, especially because the President is asking that he comes to the podium. My husband sits where he is, like a stone.

"The man is shy. He is a modest man but he was the one who brought the leaflets advertising the Outreach and I accept." The President's laugh is boisterous as he slaps his thigh. "Everyone except the very old and sick and the maimed…" (and I'm thinking that's just about everybody in this hospital of a country and this hospital life) "is to attend, whatever their religious affiliation. If you are a Muslim you must attend. If you practice native… er… spirituality you must attend." His aide whispers. "And if you belong to the Celestials or white garment churches you must attend." For clarification he repeats, "You must attend. It is my express wish that you attend. It is for your very own good."

Where is Deaconess?

Courses are served. The President has outdone himself with this fare. I should say that in his capacity as Captain of the ship of state, he has gone overboard. My intestines are not about to follow suit. It is good to be able to use pregnancy as an excuse for everything. I shall not eat the thin slivers of imported ham and melon, the creamed onion soup, the rolls of bread, the chicken with its ruched skin peeled off and the wild rice so prettily decorated with tomatoes cut in the shape of rosettes. Rosettes. Rosita. Well, perhaps a bite or two.

The President has said that every Nigerian should attend the Outreach; if anyone happens to fall ill, the President will arrange for video versions of the proceedings to be produced for that person. But the President suggests that no one should fall ill. At the Outreach, the President will make a gesture. My husband is sitting so quietly. He believes that evil will be turned to good. He knows it.

Deaconess returns. She has, I see, changed her attire. That is the usual elitist thing here. At lahdeedah functions, celebrants, particularly women, have the habit of changing three or four times. She is now clad in a silver and purple trouser suit, no longer in the traditional garb as befitting one who usually dresses in nothing else.

I'm staring so hard at her that someone says too loudly, "Aren't you Deaconess's friend? Isn't she a friend of yours? Do you know Deaconess?"

"No," I say, feeling like Peter, who said that he would rather die than betray Christ. I am thankful that, though this is night-time and I am being asked questions which I would rather not answer, my name is not Peter. I do not betray. And I do not betray the one I love more than life itself; more than myself. Betrayal can come so easily: a word, a gesture, the blink of an unseeing eye; the passing of coins from hand to hand; the high principles shattered in understanding too late; the betrayal that results in a pole of hanging until the feet twitch and the toes curl in a field which history records as a field of blood.

Deaconess has a bottle of palm wine in her hands. She announces that it has been specially tapped for the President in honour of the occasion and that the President should toast the gathering. The President announces that he prefers to wait until the dinner is over and then, in private, he and Deaconess will enjoy the palm wine. He declares that he has taken her back into his life to such an extent that there is no rift between them and she is now his chief wife and will live in the presidential compound. His senior wife is not too happy with this speech. She rises from her table and walks out. The President ignores her. He does not want a scene. I know that when I read the papers tomorrow, I will see an obituary, see the face of the senior wife there in black and white, the cause of death being noted as "died in mysterious circumstances."

I long to leave this get-together. How on earth did Deaconess expect to kill Butcher Boy by publicly poisoning him? Did she really believe that he would fall for such a ploy? Excusing myself, I go over to my husband's table. He is also relieved that pregnancy can be employed to such good effect and we begin to walk out of the hall. The President, informed of our early departure, is affable but concerned.

"Such a pity. What you need is a good rest, Madam." He attempts to shake my husband's hand. My husband fumbles with my shawl and by such intricacies of detail we actually avoid shaking the President's hand. We are ushered into the foyer where the not-so-secret army men lounge with their guns on their hips. A servant calls one of the men who is in charge of parking cars, and soon we are on our way home.

I try to make my voice sound light. "Those traitors, as Butcher Boy calls them... You remember the news when... I mean the executions at Lekki Beach... Gardener..."

"Well?"

"Gardener was among them. Gardener was shot."

"Are you sure? How do you know for certain?"

"I just know. Husband mine, please trust me."

"I hope you haven't gotten yourself involved with anything.

The President, this regime… I shouldn't have to tell you… It's a dangerous game they're playing. And you say Gardener was shot? A foolhardy, impetuous man if ever there was one. May his soul rest in peace. The times are dangerous, and the President…"

"He can't get rid of either of us that easily. One, I'm pregnant and you know how pregnant women are revered in this country. And as for you, my darling husband, you are a man of God. Butcher Boy tends to be cautious with the man upstairs."

"He pretends to be cautious. What have you been doing?"

"Trust me. I have to go over what I've written about the revolt."

"What revolt?"

"Can you please, please, trust me?"

At home we find Nurse sitting in the livingroom. Deaconess, her face covered in bruises, enters. She shows us some cigarette burns on her arm. Her dress is torn. She has been beaten up by Butcher Boy's thugs. The thugs asked Deaconess if she thought that he, the President, could be poisoned – by a woman at that. Their years of marriage, when he was a private in the army, should have shown her he was no pushover and never would be. He's said that she should come and see us and that she's under surveillance. She cannot be trusted.

Tonight I feel some dregs of sympathy for Nurse, even though she threatened to harm me with the scissors. Her fiancé, whether she loved him or not, has been shot dead, and her mother has been roughed up by her own father. Where does that leave us? Why did Butcher Boy send Deaconess to our home? Those scissors. Was Nurse just trying to scare me? The scissors are still on the chair. She sees me looking at them and begins to sob in a heart-rending way. My own heart is just about to commune with hers when – wouldn't you know? – she falls into my husband's arms. To stop her crying – and get her out of his comforting clasp – I ask her to tell me the fourth letter in the Hangman's Game. I know I'd sort of been threatened by her against playing the game, but my question has the desired effect. She unclasps herself and mumbles the correct answer.

"It is a T, Madam."

Deaconess has all the while been reigning curses on her

137

erstwhile husband. She says, "Madam, at this moment we should be thinking of how we're going to get rid of Butcher Boy. Gardener told me you agreed to help. My poor son-in-law!"

My husband shouts, "Sweetie, I warned you!"

"Someone has to kill him," Deaconess continues. "Poison is too good a death for that animal. Oh my poor misguided son-in-law…"

I ignore her and ask her daughter, "Nurse, you said T is the fourth letter in the game?"

"Yes Madam, T for trouble."

"A capital t or a common one?"

"A capital T."

"Of course, you must know by now that you're wrong. The t I'm thinking of is a common one signifying the crucifixion on the cross."

Deaconess and my husband are listening closely to this altercation. Deaconess then leaves the house without even saying goodnight. My husband tells me to go to bed and get some rest. I obviously need some. She of the shaven head, who told me I am a piece of shit and who is in so much control of herself, asks if Madam will need her further. No. Madam will not.

The last thing I want to do in this world is write. But write I must. I'm feeling the chills. Quamina had taken control, had decided to act before the appointed date of the revolt. The Demerara insurrection failed. What would happen in Nigeria? Gardener was dead, had been murdered in cold blood on Butcher Boy's orders… Who betrayed Gardener? Would there be a revolt in Nigeria? I was so tired with thinking that I fell asleep at my desk, waking up around midday annoyed with myself for having fallen asleep. And at such a time.

★ ★ ★ ★ ★

Nurse comes in to tell me that my daughter is at nursery school. My husband, thankfully, is upstairs working away on plans for the Outreach. I don't know exactly why I do so, but I tell Nurse, "I want my daughter to be collected from school right away." And yes, as I speak there is an explosion in the distance. It could not be that far away. The house shudders and one of the bulbs from the chandelier falls on the carpet. Nurse and I stand looking at the glass bulb. Through the window, I can see fires, smoke curling. My daughter is still at school. We have to go and get her. But how? I can't drive. I go upstairs and have guessed correctly. My husband is asleep over his papers.

He wakes up when I enter the room. "What's the matter? I was having a good dream."

"No time for dreaming," I say softly. "There's been an explosion, fire. Didn't you hear it? I think there's been a coup."

He looks at me as if I was the one who has been dreaming. He gets up and shouts, "Nonsense! A coup! Just before the Outreach where so many people are going to be saved! The President himself!" He *has* been dreaming. He said so himself. Downstairs Nurse has switched on the TV. The screen is rainbowed in colour. Military music strides into the living-room. She switches it off and then presses the knob of the radio. The same military music. It is the unmistakable sign that a coup has taken place. My husband collapses into a chair.

"Nurse, bring my husband a glass of water." I tell him we have to go and fetch our daughter from nursery school. When it dawns on him that she is out there and when another explosion shudders the house, he runs to the door, me following closely. We leave Nurse in the house.

The car speeds. The school is only forty minutes away. It is the longest forty minutes of my life. Soldiers with tear gas, jeeps, shooting, the kick and thrust of legs and arms running for cover. Everywhere uniformed soldiers, a oneness in their hard helmets and army boots. The city is on fire. Overturned trestles by the roadside. Dense smoke; people running; frightened eyes. Bedlam is the name of this city. The street to my daughter's school is blocked. There is a barrier of burning tyres. Soldiers prowl, their hands on their guns. This is the revolt writ large. One of the soldiers stops the car just as we are about to reverse and try another route. My husband whips out his identification card. He doesn't need it. He is recognized as a man of God. We sidle past the heat of the tyres; my heart is in my mouth.

We reach the school. There is no sign of damage on the walls. When Butcher Boy first came to power, one of his many children attended this very school. Since then, the brood, I understand, have been sent to Switzerland for "finishing" skills. Others are in England. My daughter slips through the knot of children standing by their frightened teacher. She is excited and I smile with relief. I hug her, bending down as much as I can. My baby is expected very soon. With all that's been going on in my life, in my mind and outside it, I have not given much thought to my unborn child. The other children are shouting and hooting. As she grasps my hand, her chatter takes me, lifts me up in bounds and leaps.

"Mummy, there were bombs! Teacher says there's been something called a coop." I bundle her into the car and my husband immediately backs it out of the school road and off we go. Again, the soldiers recognize us and they don't trouble us. The sky is suffused with smoke. Fires are everywhere leaping, caressing, languidly licking, demolishing buildings. I can hear the fires. Some hiss. Some roar. I know that our house is safe. It has to be, in spite of the glass chandelier that fell to the floor. Strangely, I do not feel fear. My daughter is silent. Then she says it's like a film on TV. And truly it is. An illusion, unreal, as we sit, the three of us, driving through this technicolour film. I wonder what the President is feeling at this moment in time – he who boasted of surviving so many assassination attempts because some divine will ordered it thus. I wonder how he is feeling – and his family, his wives, his hangers-on. And Deaconess. The President, it is rumoured, has an underground shelter with lots of tunnels running to it in case of times like these. Maybe he is at this moment running as fast as he can through these tunnels. When he comes out into the open, mole-like, will the eyes that have been blind for so long be dazzled by the sun? Or will he simply remain as he was? Blind? Blind as was, as is?

The last road block. These soldiers do not recognize us, my husband.

"So you are a man of God? Can God save you from this?"

It is a soldier, perhaps their leader, who speaks. He fingers his gun. My husband says nothing. They tell him to get out of the car.

My daughter is watching her father and the soldiers. I am not watching. The soldiers frisk him. He has no gun on him; no weapon of any sort. Only those impossible/possible leaflets of the coming Christian Outreach. I hope the soldier's heart will be touched by the words on those leaflets. This soldier cannot read. My husband slowly reads the words out loud for him. I am still not watching. I am rocking myself to and fro, silently praying. It is my wish now that I could speak in tongues and speak to God in a language not controlled by me. A mystery language. A heavenly language of faith connecting me. The soldier's face lights up. It is not the light of the fire which licks the buildings of this city. He has seen something we do not see. My husband has his hands held high above his head. He is a man consumed by his mission. That is all. He had no part in this revolt or that Demerara one. But the soldier barks an order. My husband is told to lie flat, face down on the ground. This he does. He lies down flat, his face to the ground. The soldier levels his gun at my husband's head and my faith fails me. I am not thinking of my daughter, numb. I am not thinking of the fires jumping higher, nearer. My wish, my hope, my prayer, is water. Baptismal water. The soldier is saying that… he is saying that the coup would not have occurred if the President had not been told about the Outreach. That it was because of the planned Outreach that some people got it into their heads that the President could be ousted.

I have to do something. I scream. "In the name of Jesus, he is not involved! In the name of Jesus!" The eyes of the soldier turn towards me as if aware of my presence for the first time. One of the other soldiers begins to plead on our behalf. The leader soldier asks some questions and the pleading soldier pleads no more. He is shot in the back and I see a torn, raggedy hole in the cloth of his jacket, a red roundness of a hole.

The leader turns again to me. "See where your God has left you? Will you continue to pray?"

There is nothing else for me to do, but pray. I decide to get out of the car.

"If you shoot him you have to shoot me."

"And your daughter?"

My daughter. Oh God, my daughter. He goes towards my

husband's body and kicks him in the side. The feet with their soldier boots kick and kick and my husband moans.

"Where is your God now? Why is he allowing this to happen to you when he loves you so much?"

My husband attempts to speak. His cheeks are swollen and the pain, my husband's pain, is tangible. The pain in him I could touch. He addresses me and my daughter, who has her thumb in her mouth. Her eyes are wide-opened. My husband, my daughter's father, the love of my life, says, "May Jesus Christ reign forever and keep us. I love you." He has given up.

I cannot give up. The soldier comes to my side of the car and strokes my stomach with his bayonet. Says his wife is pregnant. My unborn child kicks him. He laughs. "Takes after his mother!" he quips. He turns his back on us, tells the soldiers, "Let them pass."

In our haste, me now at the wheel, my husband in the back with my daughter, I discover I know how to drive. But not that smoothly. As we leave – the soldiers even saluting – I hear a crunch. Looking back, I see the arm of the dead soldier; I have driven over the bone of his outstretched hand. I say a prayer for the hand. I wish I could bury that hand in a valley of dry bones.

We arrive at our house. It is still intact. Nurse gives my husband and my daughter a sedative which will take them through the darkness of this night. I make her take one too. On the radio the military music continues. Still no word as to the whereabouts of the President. We don't know if he is still in power or not. It is imperative that I write all night. It is my only hope. I reach for the words and the pen to write them.

I decide to write the third and final section of the book: *Did you ever see such a thing in your life?* In this part I shall try to wrap things up. Quamina has been caught running away by Captain McTurkeyen. He has been executed and his head shoved on the spiked railings of Le Resouvenir Plantation as a warning to all those slaves who feel they can revolt against the government and get away with it. Before he dies, I make him see a vision of his lost children in a time that once was. After the revolt, the Governor declares a curfew in the colony. Soldiers everywhere and the streets of Georgetown piled high with bodies; many scaffolds with hundreds upon hundreds of slaves hanged, gibbeted. In the midst of this, John is arrested and charged with high treason for his alleged involvement in the revolt. Captain McTurkeyen is the one who comes to arrest him. He is unmoved when John tells him he is a man of God and therefore cannot be treated like a common criminal. McTurkeyen seizes John's diary as evidence.

John never had a hope of surviving Demerara; it wasn't only his stubborn blindness, his unwillingness to bend in any way to colonial rule; he also had a poor constitution, a weak chest. Poor John. Poor Mary. She is overcome by remorse for her part in planning the women's revolt and feels guilt, bitterness against everyone when John is arrested and tried. John accepts his lot with stoic calm. He knows that his end is near. I see him listening with wonder to the list of crimes against the state which he was supposed to have committed. Mary is in the courtroom watching, listening...

* * * * *

A clanking noise. Metal against metal. A shuffle of slave feet shoeless on the courtroom floor. The building so packed that many were forced to stand, backs pressed against the walls. Heads turned to see a line of slaves manacled and chained to each other, a connecting chain between neck and neck. Body and body. Slave and slave. They were followed by others, men who wore top hats and ill-fitting buckra clothing. Mary recognized Samuel, Aggie clad in a satin gown, Bristol… He dared not look at John. Her John.

What would she do if John was sentenced to hang? When Captain McTurkeyen and the militia men broke down the door, when they tied John's hands behind his back, when they barked their soldier words: "High Treason. You, John Smithers, are charged with High Treason, an offence punishable by hanging", John had been so very silent and in his silence there was a beauty of surrender so pure she too was astonished into silence. She would look at him, however much it hurt.

There he sits, my John, his head bowed. He is so innocent and it is his innocence which has brought him to this dock. He is so thin. I can see the neckbones under his skin and they jag their splinters into my heart. The prosecutor – all breeches, boots, epaulettes – strides towards John, bends to speak to him. He walks to the table at the front of the courtroom. It is stacked with papers, files, evidence, incriminating words which seek to kill my John. John's diary, confiscated by McTurkeyen, is on the table. McTurkeyen sits by the Governor's chair. At the table sit a Lieutenant-Colonel Who of this regiment and Captain What of that regiment and soldiers, soldiers. Pearsons and Gruegel eye me behind their fluttering fans which whisper loud. The Governor has arrived and he walks slowly to the chair reserved for him. Everyone rises. Bodies stiff, the hands of the presiding officers raised in salute and the lone trumpet strident.

Rule Britannia
Britannia rules the waves
Britons never never never
Shall be slaves

Eyes on Mary. The only one sitting. Whispers. Then loud talk. The Governor shouting "Order!"

Order.

John should not be tried by martial law. In the history of the colonies this has never been done. This is a charade, a game to them.

Ring a ring of roses
A pocket full of posies
Atishoo! Atishoo!
We all fall down
Down

The prosecutor was speaking and she should listen.

"…indeed, John Smithers, from the moment he stepped onto the shores of Demerara, was already plotting to sabotage the state, employing God's word as a religious cloak to hide his designs. This… this fomenter of sedition…"

"Proceed," instructed the Governor.

"Pardon me, Your Excellency. The charges against Smithers are such that I shudder to think that one of our kind, an Englishman, a man of the cloth, should have…"

"Proceed, what!"

"Smithers on his arrival in the colony of Demerara was given specific instructions against teaching our slaves to read and write – pursuits that promote sloth and laziness – and yet, being of stubborn temperament, over the years the so-called pastor of Bethel Chapel repeatedly contravened colonial authority, the authority of His Excellency, Governor Murrain, the authority of his most Gracious Majesty, the King, and actively, and brazenly did so… in teaching the slaves to read and write. Mr. Hamilblade, the overseer of Le Resouvenir Plantation where Smithers resided, has already testified to this end."

The man, his arm bandaged, nodded and smiled at the prosecutor.

"Smithers' wanton disregard for the law was also reflected in what I shall refer to as the Sunday issue. The Sabbath is a sacred, holy day of rest. When God in his infinite wisdom decided to make Sunday holy, He had a plan. Sunday was created for men, not animals, chattel. Yet

145

the misguided pastor of Bethel Chapel insisted that his slave congregation attend services on Sunday whether or not their labour was required by their masters. In so doing he abjured the wishes of the state and preached that even when the cane needed to be brought in and field work attended to, that the slaves should... In short, my friends, Smithers sought to transform the slaves into men and thereby subvert the entire institution of slavery sanctioned by God Himself. Did not Apostle Paul send Onesimus, a slave who stole his master's goods and ran away from him, back to his master Philemon and to slavery once more?

"It is well known that the nature of the African is to be indolent. Smithers, in his bid to undermine the directives of the state, in his resolution that the slaves practise Christianity according to his own dictates... Well, my friends, as we know, the actions and words of Smithers led to disastrous consequences for all of us in this colony.

"At this juncture I call the witness, Aggie... You are Aggie, slave at the Governor's Residence?"

"Yes, Massa."

"In your own words tell the court what John Smithers said to you concerning this Sunday issue."

Aggie, her voice low: "Reverend Massa Smithers say... he say we mustn't do work 'pon Sunday."

"Aggie, you may step down."

"Let the court know that these letters were written to the prisoner... In them Smithers was told..."

"Get to the revolt. Get to the revolt," the Governor interjected. The British Empire's time and money lavished on a nincompoop! It was simple. The man had obviously incited these savage heathen to rebellion. He should be hanged.

"Yes, your Excellency." The prosecutor bowed, tugging at the lapels of his jacket.

"I shall now draw the court's attention to the circumstances which led directly to the revolt.

"Just prior to the rebellion, Smithers preached a sermon entitled 'Fight the good fight of faith', taken from the Book of Romans. Indeed, he exhorted his slave congregation with some of the most injudicious sentiments espoused in the Bible, advising the Negroes for instance, and I quote, 'To put on the whole armour'. Later he preached from the Book of Exodus which details Moses leading and delivering the Israelites from Egyptian slavery. It is the belief of this court that John Smithers preached these sermons with evil intent, with the knowledge that, like children, the blacks would be inflamed, discontented with their lot, and would, as did in fact occur, revolt.

"Children, ladies and gentlemen, children. The Negroes are little more than children. They rely on us for food, shelter, for protection. Their minds, their very sensibilities, are not as developed as ours and it is clear that this man, this so-called pastor of the Christian faith, has preyed upon, nay, infused the minds of these black children, instilled treasonous, rebellious desires in their hearts. The Negro species lacks intellect; they are a race who cannot think for themselves. Can we be surprised, then, that when placed under the influence of a man like Smithers they should aspire to rebellion? Aspirations which led to the disastrous occurrences of March 23rd, the day of the revolt?

"It is quite conceivable that Smithers insinuated that he himself was the Moses who would lead the slaves to freedom. Our slaves cannot be expected to fathom the intricacies, nuances of the Word of God… It is far too sophisticated for them. And yet it is the Word of God that Smithers entrusted to his Chief Deacon, Quamina, the executed rebel, in so-called 'after teachings' to the slaves wherein Quamina interpreted not the Bible, but the bible of John Smithers.

"Quamina himself, as Captain McTurkeyen discovered, was given certain pamphlets on the Abolition of slavery, speeches by the Honourable Mr. Wilberforce and Mr. Canning who, not having encountered the bestial animality of the slaves, cannot be expected to know better; Quamina, ladies and gentlemen, was presented with these highly incendiary notions by John Smithers. For what purpose, I ask you? For what purpose would a man of God give these papers to a slave, his Chief Deacon?"

Tears on Rosita's face. It was she who had given Quamina the pamphlets – the tracts her mistress gave her after she had cut off her hair. Quamina had asked her why the shorn head and she had presented him with the pamphlets and…

"It is our submission that Smithers, if he did not directly orchestrate the revolt, certainly knew that rebellion was afoot. Many of the insurgents belong to his congregation. He is their pastor, privy to their innermost desires and as such he knew of their intention to rise against the most gracious person of our sovereign, the King."

"Proceed, proceed," rumbled the Governor, unbuttoning his fly under the table. Discreetly. "Proceed."

"On the evening following the uprising, when we were uncertain as to the extent to which the prisoner had colluded with the insurgents, Captain McTurkeyen personally visited Smithers at Plantation Le Resouvenir and informed him that it was his duty as a subject of the Crown to enrol in the militia. Smithers stated that as a pastor he could not be expected to serve in the militia, or presumably, serve his country and the British Empire in its time of need."

Witness after witness lied against John. There was Bristol. There was Philomena from Montrose. There was Tyndal from Bachelor's Adventure. There was Paris from Felicity. There was Goodluck from as far away as Ruimveldt Plantation. Voices. Voices. A concert of voices, unctuous and cloying.

And John. His wrists and ankles manacled like a slave, his head lowered and yes, a peace in him as he sat. Against the accusations, deceit, lies, he did not open his mouth. Reverend John Smithers – the reverence fled it seemed to some – but for others the reverence in him spoke eloquently. They saw the manacles around his limp wrists and wondered how the bright metal circles shone incandescent, luminous, imbued with something higher. Rosita saw, knew and understood. She cast a sidelong glance at Mary listening intently to the prosecutor.

"I very much doubt it, but there may be colonists among us who believe that because the prisoner has refused either to employ the services of a lawyer or indeed defend himself against the charges brought before him... there may be some who deem us unjust. That, ladies and gentlemen, is not the British way. If any harbour such sympathy with the prisoner, I ask that person to step out of this courtroom and see the outcome of this most heinous of crimes. The majority of the buildings in Georgetown are burnt; many of our women folk have had to be shipped to contiguous areas; some of us have lost friends and relatives butchered by the cutlass, or shot by the muskets of rebellious slaves. Had it not been for the decisive measures which His Excellency Governor Murrain took, his sagacity in sending his officers to the East Coast to stockade and hang the slaves as soon as he suspected a revolt was in the making, the uprising would have had even graver consequences. As it is, in the future, His Majesty is to assign no less than twelve hundred troops – two complete regiments – and two vessels of war to be constantly kept on the station.

And ladies – I deeply regret, Mrs. Gruegel, the fate of your beloved husband – you ladies who have courageously remained in Georgetown need no longer be overly concerned about your physical or spiritual safety. From henceforth, proper restrictions on the transit of missionaries to British Guiana are to be effected that we might guard against the risk of evilly disposed persons coming to these colonies in a position which gives them so much influence over the minds of the Negroes."

The prosecutor was not done yet. His hands on John's diary – the one Mary had given him – on the table and covered in dust. So many slaves to dust tables and they had not cleared it of dust. Dust and ashes. Dust to dust. Ashes to ashes. And beauty for ashes. Perhaps.

"And as the reading of Smithers' diary shall prove, the accused…"

Smithers prayed. With every beat of his heart he prayed. Let me not have written about my love for Rosita. Even in this place, thoughts catch in his throat about wanting to and not wanting to love her, knowing that he should not love her, but struggling to suppress that desire over the years… They were going to hang him again with the noose of his diary. These thoughts brought on a coughing fit, and a spatter of blood sprayed his torn shirt…

Let me not have written. Let Mary not know. Let her not hear. God, my father, even with the knowing that I shall soon be with you, my mission done… I implore you, my God, I entreat you, let Mary not know. Spare her this last pain.

The prosecutor and the killing words. Relentless.

"…is an immoral man. A man not fit to be a pastor, an Englishman. As these extracts from his diary shall reveal, his moral turpitude is such that he involved himself…"

"I is for the defence. I is for Reverend Massa John. And is talk I going talk. You call yourself gentlemen! You, the buckra. You say you fair and talk talk bout British justice and thing… Let go me hand! I going talk!"

It was Auntie Lou who had pushed her way through the courtroom and stood before the Governor.

"Very well, very well. We are British. We are fair. She can give evidence if she so chooses."

The prosecutor, John's diary in his hand, clamped it shut. What were things coming to! Just as he was about to conclude the proceedings and pronounce his judgement, this huge black woman invades the courtroom and instead of being thrown out is allowed by the Governor to speak. It was no wonder that the colony had...

"What are you waiting for, my good man? Get on with it!"

"You are Auntie Lou of..."

"I is Louise," announced Auntie Lou folding her arms. She had never seen so many buckra in one place at one time. The court was filled to capacity. Apart from selected witnesses, no slaves were permitted to attend the trial – a white man in the dock. Not seemly, what! the Governor had said. Some slaves had nonetheless straggled away from their plantations and as the hours passed, their numbers outside the courthouse had grown. Auntie Lou had seen despair, concentration wrapped around their faces like tight cloths.

"I say I is Louise. Ask me question. Pretend you asking me question in the name of British justice and ask me bout Reverend Massa John. You all hang him already, so ask me."

The prosecutor stared at Governor Murrain. Surely now in the light of such audacity – a common Negro slave – the Governor would give the order to have her thrown out? But there he sat, porcine, his absent eyebrows bulging. Could it be that he feared this woman, this slave?

Auntie Lou began to sing. The slaves were well acquainted with the hymn.

"Onward Christian soldiers marching as to war."

"You will be silent, Auntie Lou!" At last the Governor spoke.

"With the cross of Jesus..."

"Auntie Lou, stop it I say, or, or, it is the stocks for you."

"Going on before..."

"You will soon be in contempt of court!"

"Christ the royal master..."

"You will be whipped if you persist with this nonsense!"

"Leads against the foe..."

The Governor brought down his mallet so forcibly it almost splintered the table.

"Alright, I true sorry, Massa Govna, sah, if I did do anything to vex you sah." Auntie Lou has her hand on the cover of a Bible.

The prosecutor, disgust in his tone: "Do you solemnly swear to tell the truth, the whole truth and nothing but the truth, so help you God?"

"Christian can't swear."

"Swear, goddamit!" shouted Governor Murrain.

"You want me to swear to God or to you? I have to know before I swear."

"Just swear," commanded the Governor. "You are helping neither yourself nor Smithers with such insubordination."

She had heard the word before. The Governor had said "insubordination" when she had broken his chamber pot. Then he had had her beaten with the cat-o-nine. The bruises had not healed. She had heard of insubordination before and it made her laugh and when she laughed the Governor involuntarily drew back his chair, then suddenly slumped, tired. Tired with everything.

She was up on her feet walking towards him, standing before him, the Governor of the colony of Demerara. Tearing off her bandana, she flung it to the floor. It was a gesture inherited without thought from a continent, hers, across the seas.

Governor Murrain watched her. In all the years since he had known Auntie Lou, he had never seen her head, her hair without the bandana. The movement, the very hair of her head, unsettled him. It was a well-formed head, the black curls threaded with white. She seemed ten years younger, her face in relief almost girlish, so that when he listened to her vitriolic speech, the contrast between face and talk made him gasp with the knowledge that he had never known her. How she felt, what she thought; what – he winced – she thought of him.

"This thing you all call trial is stupid nonsense." She pointed to John. "All you already convict he. You want talk justice and British Empire and King George and God in you donkey breath… You beat us like animals, you buy slave tongue because you make us fear you, the buckra. You think cause we black we stupid, and you think because the revolt didn't work out we stupid and we like children like that pipsqueak prosecutor say. A boy like he talking bout man and woman as if we children! Well let me tell you something. I don't fear you buckra. Governor, King George, prosecutor… not one of all you. You

151

whip me before not so? It make me feel bad, but not because the lash cut me skin... Since time when you put chain on another buckra like you own self and you all say he did high treason thing, I don't fear you. High treason is what you all do to we! High treason my ass! I been laughing at all you. You in know that this going be last slave revolt this Demerara going see. When a see you put white man like you own self in the stocks and lie gainst him I know slavery over and I free. And you Govna... you..."

It was the soldier by the Governor's right who dragged Auntie Lou into the courtyard where she stood her full height and spat into the dust.

"Suspend proceedings," Murrain spluttered. The assembly began to file out leaving John sitting in the dock almost forgotten. Inside, too, the Governor sat, his flies undone.

★ ★ ★ ★ ★

"Madam, did you call me?"

Nurse. Her eyes red from weeping.

"No I didn't call you."

"I'm sorry, Madam. Sorry for…"

"Try to take things easy. I know your fiancé has, has… You will see everything will turn out alright…"

"Madam, I think I know the next letter for the word in the game. It's R isn't it?"

"R for what?" I ask guardedly.

"R for rebirth?" She's right, but I don't mind her getting this particular letter. It belongs to me too. And besides, that cross she wears around her neck is quite a nice cross. It must mean she's not the reprobate I thought she was. She's looking so unattractive with those red eyes and that shaven head.

Someone at the door.

"Yes. Who is it?"

"We come on the President's orders." I have heard that voice before. Shaking, I get up from my chair. My feet are pins and needles. I stamp them and gain some measure of courage from the act. A song comes to my mind. "Whenever I feel afraid I hold my head up high and whistle a happy tune and no one ever knows I'm afraid. *The King and I*. It is, I think, *The President and I*. I move to the door. For some reason I am drawn to the feet of those who knock. They are shod in the usual regulation army boots. The wrought-iron burglar bars and several padlocks are between me and them. I fumble with the keys, trying to buy time. The soldier who stands in front of the four who come with him has an exasperated look on his face and he reaches for his revolver and expertly shatters the padlocks one by one. I duck to avoid the bullets. He grins. I recognize him. He is the same soldier who wanted to shoot my husband at the roadblock. He has wide handlebar whiskers that escaped my notice before.

They enter my living room and I watch the tread of the imprinting boot-marks on my carpet. When they take their seats I continue to gaze at the carpet and the puncture holes from their boots.

"Where is your husband?"

"He is upstairs, sleeping in the bedroom."

I tell Nurse to go and wake him.

"What have you been doing today?" asks the soldier.

"Writing."

He grins at his fellow-soldiers. One of them has opened our drinks cabinet and is pouring himself a glass of our best whiskey. He sees me looking at him and asks if there is any beer in the house. I point to the kitchen and they leave in a body, except for their leader, who sits upright in a chair, his hands on either side of the arm-rests, palms down.

"Go and get your husband!"

It is a command which I am in no position to refuse, but I do. "He's sleeping. I've given him a sedative. He'll be of no use to you. My nurse is probably trying to wake him up. Why do you want to see him?"

"Why, Madam? Your husband is needed at headquarters for questioning."

"What for? He hasn't done anything."

"I'm sure he hasn't, but I must follow my orders."

I have to stall. I have no intention of them leaving this house with my husband. But I climb the stairs slowly and enter our bedroom. Nurse has obviously abandoned the attempt to wake him. She is nowhere to be seen. My husband was so exhausted he hadn't bothered to change and is lying fully clothed on the bed. I go back down the stairs and face the quizzical eyebrows of the soldier.

"Well, Madam, where is he?"

"He has to get dressed."

The soldiers are still in the kitchen. They are now eating the contents of the fridge.

Their leader says. "I understand you are writing a novel.

What's it about? It hasn't got an outreach in it... as part of the plot?"

I sit down in my chair, frantically wondering if an outreach occurred in Demerara.

"It's a historical novel. It has to do with the last slave insurrection which happened in Demerara. It happened in 1823."

"Insurrection?" he asks snidely. "I don't suppose there is a deaconess, a gardener, a nurse-maid, and a very reverend gentleman behind the insurrection?"

"I don't know what you mean," I say haltingly.

"Madam," the whiskers drawl, "I know your game. I was one of the officers who executed your gardener and…"

When he says "game" I stifle my fear and ask this soldier, "Perhaps you'd like to think of a letter representing a certain word I'm thinking of…."

He is amused. He believes I am really playing a game.

"The clue is the most mighty ruler in Africa and the world itself."

"Your husband is taking a long time. I respect you. I don't want to have to get him out of bed myself. You wouldn't like that, would you?"

"Have you thought of the letter? To my clue?"

"Why it is the President, of course. The only letter you can be thinking of is P. P for President."

I smile and then I laugh boisterously and in so unladylike a fashion that a beer-drunken soldier pops his head round the kitchen door.

"Am I right? I am right, aren't I?" he prompts.

"No, you're wrong. The letter is O for Omnipotent. For God."

He stares at me. "You do realize, of course, Madam, that what you have just said could be construed as a treasonable offence? The President is the greatest ruler of Nigeria and the world… God doesn't come into the equation in any way."

Now it's me staring at him and me who might be arrested. The way he's looking at me I know my husband will not be arrested like John in Demerara, and sent for questioning. The soldier with the whiskers knows my game. I do believe he knows. It seems as if this man is giving me some sort of choice. It's either I agree with him that Butcher Boy is more powerful than God and become a slave to that belief, or I disagree with him and tell him the truth that God is omnipotent and the leader of Nigeria and the world. And become a slave to God? A choice of slaveries. Maybe I should have called the novel of my life, "A choice of slaveries". A choice of life or death. I choose life. With my free will I choose to be God's slave and live. I am not afraid of death. To think that this soldier here should have been the one to bring me to this truth of the Hangman's Game. A choice of slaveries. Not caring about death because of the life hereafter. The cross. Uncaring and free.

"Madam," he says, "Who do you believe is the greatest ruler in the world, the President or God?"

"God."

"I could have you shot... both you and your baby."

"You could. But you won't."

He stretches his legs out with the lazy ease of a man who is in control of my life.

"You are an interesting woman, and though I am absolutely sure that you, your husband, Deaconess... yes Deaconess and her daughter were behind the coup, which, incidentally, the God you serve did nothing to prevent... The President is still in power... I'm going to put you all under house arrest." He pauses. "I think it's a reasonable alternative to execution for treason against the state of Nigeria, don't you?"

"Am I supposed to answer that?"

"And the reason for my clemency lies not with God. I have no fear of God or man... My loyalties, such as they are... Madam, I was one of your husband's students at the university and your husband was a fair man, good to me. That's the only reason ..."

"Why thank you, officer," I say meekly, although I'm longing to be sarcastic and tell him that God, before the creation of the world, made my husband his teacher at the university.

I look past him in the direction of the kitchen and he rises.

"Next time you might not be so lucky."

When the last of the army boots have stamped their way out I know I should sleep. I drag my feet to the kitchen and look with dismay at the aftermath of the soldiers' visit: torn bread, opened cans of corned beef, a sack of rice stranded on the floor, broken beer bottles… I close my eyes to the scene and hurriedly make myself a cup of strong black coffee. I return to my novel; didn't know I could be so confident.

Back to the novel. John is still under arrest and given his wretched quarters and his poor health he is very weak and on the point of death. And Mary… My poor Mary mine…

* * * * *

John was going to die. They were going to hang him with his red hair and those words of his and God's. I wonder if they ever make ropes out of paper and words in a kind of hangman's game? Or are the ropes made from rope only? For that is the death the Governor and his trumped-up tribunal have chosen. A death by hanging. There he will be and they will cover his face, John's face, with a dark bag so that he will see only darkness before the light. I wonder if ropes can be made of letters or of words and hair hanging so closely together that they form a noose which, when tightened, strangles with a crush of splintering neckbone?

God, won't you forgive me and allow me sleep to balm the hurt of my mind? It was my Rapunzel-braided rope of hair that John refused to climb to plant kisses on my mouth, which wanted only kisses freely given... It was that which led him to this dock and time. It was that, wasn't it, God? Father in heaven, may your will be done. But please let them not hang him. Spare his life and forgive me for my sins. Let him not hang. Let help come. Oh God. Dear God, let John not hang. That's what McTurkeyen said they'd do to him. That's what McTurkeyen said.

★ ★ ★ ★ ★

At last… McTurkeyen. Let me see what he's all about.

*****

What was it that drew him, Captain McTurkeyen, to John Smithers' cell? He rode hard, the horse under him as her screams were under him on that night when Quamina saw. It was not the first time the animal in him had ventured out. Most times he could control it, this need to dominate and see the limbs parted and smell the flesh of another diet so strangely alien it compelled and nauseated. The crimp crush of hair, which sprang at the touch, buttocks not flat but humped – ledges that enticed but which he felt smothered in... Until that night in an empty house and a slave girl bringing him tea on a tray. They had shattered, the cups, when he pulled her to him. It was the frightened cries. Yes, that was it. It was the voice calling for help from a God he was sure did not exist. The "God help me!" and the "In the name of God!" and the shaking black fingers sketching the cross in mid-air even as she lay on his bed. It must have been that. This sketching of the cross and the calling to a God who had brought her to the colony and to this bed so that he could enter her and show that there was no God.

If God was as good as the missionaries said, he wouldn't have allowed that night, that slave, he wouldn't have allowed him to enter her and smell the odour of a diet not his. He had slapped her and she had remained quiet throughout the act. Not even a whimper. He had strapped the slave girl to the bed – the same way he had strapped that English slut to a hospital bed when he was a medical doctor, when they forced him to quit the medical profession. Forced him to change from Doctor to Captain. Malpractice was what they said. That night. That night of an empty house and a black servant girl with crimped hair which sprang to the touch of his strong hands never leaves him. When he is drinking tea he is reminded. He drinks tea every morning. It must be this that drew him to John Smithers. John Smithers, a dead man. And he, McTurkeyen, another

160

dead man. He did not even know her name. His usual manservant, an old man, had been poorly and had sent the girl up to him, he who refused to be enticed into the animality of the slaves. Beasts. Beasts of burden they were. It must have been this. For he could not have been McTurkeyen without this stamping out of those ledge-like buttocks and the odour which enticed and repelled. He could not have performed his civic duty to the Empire without this stamping out. And he had. Until that night.

The girl had died. She was buried by Quamina, who was also dead. And John Smithers was dying. Typical of Britain to send a man like Smithers to Demerara. Especially after the Berbice revolt. You'd think they'd know better.

But how could they with their Whitehall pronouncements? Manumission. The abolition of slavery. The girl, the slave girl was dead and buried by Quamina, also now dead.

His horse beneath him, Captain McTurkeyen cantered the last few miles to the house where John Smithers lay dying in a cell. He still did not know what propelled him there.

When he saw John in that rat-infested room, the planks of floorboards slimed green, the walls sagging with dampness, when he saw John's peace, the luminous light about him and in him as he drew his last breath on this Demerara earth, McTurkeyen's hands reached out in yearning. The Reverend John Smithers was dead, and he hadn't told him about the letter.

* * * * *

She held the letter in her hands. The envelope had been torn open and she regarded the royal seal of red wax, the coat of arms of King George, His Royal Majesty.

"Mistress Mary, I took the liberty of opening the missive… Good news." He attempted a smile. "Won't you sit down?" It wasn't the first time she had been present in this office. Slowly she dragged the chair backwards.

"A drink of water, my good lady?"

She removed the cream embossed paper from its envelope and read: *From the office of His Majesty the King on this day of Royal Pardon for the Mischievious crime of the Reverend John Smithers*. Sentence revoked. John Smithers to leave the colony of Demerara. Return to England. Withdraw from London Missionary Society. Sentence revoked.

The Governor watched her.

"Of course, my good woman, this has come a little late, but at least your husband's honour has been, in a sense, restored, what?"

Mary replaced the letter in its envelope. "I think, Governor Murrain, that I shall have that glass of water if you don't mind."

A steward materialized, holding a tray with a glass and napkins neatly folded by the side.

"How did you know I wanted you? Oh well, never mind. Pour the good lady a glass of water and leave us."

"Governor Murrain, may I have some more water? It's so refreshing at this time of day. It's always so hot in Demerara. I never have quite gotten used to the heat."

The woman was clearly distracted. The whole business of the revolt and the death of that rascal Smithers had quite unhinged her. Obviously she was not suited to life out here. Can't understand how she could have gotten so entangled with a man like that, even going so far as to marry the fellow. Women were like that. They never knew what they wanted and when they thought that they did, they generally chose trash. Has a bit of spunk in her, though. Loyal to the last, giving her husband succour when he most needed it and even trying to say that she had instigated the rebellion. But mad. Mad as a hatter. Knew it from the day I first met her. Should be advised to leave the colony. With her feeble mind, she won't be able to face the ostracization she's bound to get. Why, she hasn't a friend left. That's what comes from assisting beasts, blacks, no matter how well intentioned you are.

The Governor attempted gallantry. "I don't think anyone of our kind ever gets used to the heat. We tolerate it, but never, never get used to it." As if in affirmation, he began to sweat and hastily mopped his face as he tried to avert his gaze from Mary, who was sitting bolt upright.

Got to get the woman out of here. Any moment now one of his officers might come in. See him with Smithers' wife. Think him soft. And he knew his black steward was listening by the door. Like children, the blacks. With the curfew and the militia out in full force, order had been restored. Soldiers everywhere with their guns. But burnt buildings everywhere.

162

"Water cold enough for you, Mrs. Smithers?"

"Thank you, sir. The water is cold enough. Quite."

She sipped again, put the glass on the desk. The Governor noted the dryness of her eyes and felt somewhat disappointed. He had secretly hoped for some female show of tears, had expected gratitude. Her husband's sentence had been revoked. But she sat in the chair, stiff-backed, resolute in her grief. Governor Murrain, overcome by a certain chivalry, eased himself up from behind his desk and walked a few paces towards Mary.

"Governor Murrain, this is a tidy office. You have, your slaves I should say, have kept it well for you. My compliments."

"Why, thank you, dear lady. Well my good woman, if that will be all… I have a number of duties to attend to."

"Yes, I'm sure you do, Governor Murrain."

"Perhaps you could finish up your water and go home and have a rest, what?"

"Home?" Her eyes ranged around the room before alighting on him.

The woman was demented. This is not the climate for an English woman. How to make her leave the room? It would be unseemly, ungentlemanly, to get the slaves to take her out. Poor woman. Fancy saying that she coerced the slaves along with Auntie Lou and Rosita into leading a slave revolt! The very idea! Mad as a hatter. The ways of women.

"Mistress Mary, I will have to ask you to leave now. I hope that you feel ah, better. At least your late husband has been pardoned. Had he lived, his death sentence would have been revoked."

"Governor Murrain, you are too kind."

At least he was able to do some good. He had had no intention of harming the little woman.

"I had to go to a lot of trouble to get your husband pardoned, I can tell you."

"Thank you Governor Murrain. If my husband were alive he might have shown his gratitude."

Governor Murrain smiled in farewell, but when he felt the soft hand suddenly hard on his face, his absent eyebrows bulged in disbelief.

"Forgive me, Governor Murrain, the revolt, my husband's death… these things have quite unhinged my mind."

The old black slave smiled behind the closed door.

*****

They wanted him dead. John wanted to be dead. He is happier dead. Had the pardon come in time he would not have been martyred, as he is now, as he lies in the coffin on a donkey cart. As we walk to the grave. The slaves have made him a martyr. God has made him a martyr.

They did not want a funeral. They feared another revolt. They feared death. I, too, have been afraid of death. Of seeing hangings and black bodies piled high. I was, at first, afraid.

With John, I see not body only, but spirit. Spirit which moved him to shed tears, to laughter and anger; gone to another place, leaving the shell of body behind. It is for the after that I shall try to live, the ever after.

The soil has been dug though the hole is shallow. Why did I allow Rosita to come here? If it hadn't been for her... If it hadn't been for them. But I must blame myself.

The earth is soft and good for eating. I am so sorry for what I have done. They must not hear my grief, which breaking takes my speech. Here is the earth; it is for eating. But first, I must dig another hole in the ground to hide myself, my tearing heart. My fingers dig the soil in a long tunnel of dank, dark earth and I put my head in it and I scream into the hollow tunnel of moist earth.

I know that they are watching the contrary Mary and not the Mary who saw the dead body of Christ transformed, the Mary who first spoke of the good news: the stone boulder removed and the resurrection of life. I know they think me mad; even the donkey thinks so. The donkey has forgotten his testament of bearing Christ triumphant through the gates of Jerusalem.

I have not forgotten and now with the hosannas of palm leaves laid out on the ground, I can eat this earth.

*****

And I'm crying for my Mary-me. I'm thinking that had it not been for the Word and the words, there but for the Grace of God go I. We are under house arrest and Butcher Boy, for all our connivance, is alive. He has declared a curfew not only in Lagos but throughout the republic – in Enugu, Onitsha, Jos, Kano, Ibadan – everywhere. Just like the Governor in Demerara.

* * * * *

There were other letters stamped with the imperious seal of the royal Court, but this particular letter looked different. He had to retain his composure. The colony, the Empire depended upon it. Depended on him. The happenings of the past few months would have unnerved any man.

He read through the various documents that he had allowed to pile up. He appended his signature to some and decided to take this letter with the royal seal to his mansion where he would open it with his favourite penknife, not this one – this knife that had caused him so much trouble – the knife that had opened the envelope telling of the manumission for the slaves.

The Governor threw the offending implement in his waste-paper basket and rang the bell, called for his carriage, and was driven through the silent streets of Georgetown with their grim reminder of the worst days the colony had ever seen. It was hard to believe; it had all quite weakened him and he felt exhausted. People were beginning to give him curious looks – even Captain McTurkeyen, who was talking of leaving the colony. Pearsons, too, he had caught staring at him in a way which quite discomfited him. It was no way to look at a superior, at the Governor of the colony of Demerara.

Sitting on his verandah, he called a boy. His slaves, he discovered – those whom he had positioned by the doors – had been listening to his conversations with Pearsons, Gruegel, McTurkeyen. The black bastards.

"Where is Auntie Lou, what?"

"She not here."

"Go and get me the knife in the study."

The slave boy's eyes are alarmed.

"It's a small knife. You will find it in the…"

He would perform the task himself. Auntie Lou was never where she should be. The woman was becoming more and more of a nuisance. Why, it was often difficult to talk to her these days. This business about the abolition of the whipping of the little hussies had turned her head. And that rumpus at the trial when she dared to speak for Smithers and had to be thrown out of court... The woman should be given another whipping and he would be the man to do it. He walked from the verandah through the living room and into his study where he picked up the small pocketknife. Its blade was sharp, its handle made of smooth ivory. Governor Murrain cursed softly when he realized that he had forgotten the letter. He felt like sleeping. Letter first. Sleeping after.

Back on the verandah he rocked himself for a few moments before slitting the envelope with the knife blade and extracting the letter. His face became clammy as he read its contents. It couldn't be true. After so many years of service to the King in Demerara... Not this. Dismissal. Instructed to return to England on the next ship. Why should he accept this decision? He was Governor Murrain. The Governor of the colony of Demerara. He had to be collected in his thoughts. Placing the letter on the table beside him, he rang the bell. The boy who had answered earlier, appeared again.

"I rang for Auntie Lou! I rang for Auntie Lou! Haven't you nincompoops found her yet? The woman is getting above herself!"

The boy stuttered and began to back away. "Sir, sir I, I never find her."

"Come to think of it, I've not seen you before! Where are my slaves?"

"Sah," the boy blabbered, "Auntie Lou gone somewhere."

The Governor looked around for something to throw at the boy but energy drained out of him. "Leave my sight! Never, do you hear me, never enter this house again, and if you don't return with Auntie Lou I'll make sure you'll never walk again!"

The boy was puzzled.

"Get out!" the Governor bawled. "Get out I say!"

"Please Massa Govna, sah, I should come back or, or what?"

Then the Governor saw what he had been looking for; a heavy paperweight to throw at the child. The boy saw the raised hand and fled. Governor Murrain continued to rock, rock in his rocking chair, his words "Get out! Get out!" echoing as the chair rocked forwards and backwards.

"Where is Auntie Lou?"

★ ★ ★ ★ ★

Where indeed? The Governor is still alive. And so is Butcher Boy. The Governor has been dismissed from the colony of Demerara for his mishandling of the insurrection and he is going to pack his things with the help of some slaves and set sail on the next available ship for England. His Nigerian counterpart, Butcher Boy, has managed to foil the attempted coup and he is still in power. But I have a feeling things are not what they seem. Nigeria is in a bad state. Its peoples won't stand for much more of Butcher Boy's reign of terror. He had better be careful. Whatever happens in Demerara, Butcher Boy had better be careful.

* * * * *

"Careful, children. Don't fall over and get bruises."

They would soon be too tired for anything but a good night's sleep.

Speaking to the sky and the clouds passing over, speaking to the rose in her hand and the surrounding trees, the cottage behind a white picket fence, Mary thought of what might have been, of John, and wondered if he was looking down at her from heaven, and if his hair was still red, and whether he was truly happy that his cough, the slaves and Demerara had left him. As his body died, he told her of his love… his skin so thin that the light shone through, Adamic, naked.

Helen bounded to her side and snatched the rose. The thorns bit into her flesh and she smiled at the tiny pinpoints of blood on her fingers.

"Mother! Come and catch me. See if you can get the rose!" the girl cried as she ran.

"Helen, Helen, what did you call me?"

The London Missionary Society had helped her. Because of John's death they had helped her. She must be thankful. She was thankful. John's mission in Demerara had attracted some sourness to their organization but they had given her this cottage in the woods – a fairy-tale cottage with thatched roof and tiny sugary windows. And they had given her this garden in which to plant seeds, which would yield flowers like those that had already grown in the depths of her heart – like the flower Rosita, with her petal-tender face – to staunch the grief in her and give her the peace that passeth all understanding.

God would forgive and did.

This garden is a garden of Mary and I shall plant contrary seeds and from them grow. I am to spend the rest of my days here. The London Missionary Society will send me more orphan children from the slums and I will teach them how to sew and how to read and to write. And I shall teach them about travelling to distant lands where people are the same though different. Flowers shall grow in this garden. Flowers of children's lives.

Occasionally, on the days when summer had not yet passed away, she would walk to the flower beds and water them with her tears. Some who saw her would think, "There is Mary Smithers, contrary Mary. Her mind is deranged as a result of the happenings in Demerara." But those who knew her would see a woman who sang magnificats to her bed of flowers, her knees bent in supplication. They would think, the kind ones, Mary is not so contrary. Quite.

    "Mother!" It was Helen again. The child was irrepressible.
    "You promised to tell us a bedtime story."
    Mary smiled. Her charges were tucked up in bed.
    "Yes, I did promise."
    Before she tells the children, her children, a story, she unlooses her hair with its luxurious cascading length.

PART THREE

SIGHT

"I don't believe you."

"It's true, God's name be praised!"

"It's not possible… Just like that? And there I was thinking everything was a game when things had been planned every inch of the way. Is it really true?"

"Turn on the radio, the TV; listen for yourself."

I do as my husband requests and our new head of state, dressed in military uniform, blinks steadily into our livingroom as his speech comes stunning home. He had been imprisoned by Butcher Boy but he'd been so popular Butcher Boy had not dared to kill him. In prison he had become a born-again Christian and had given his life to Christ. He was also a farmer, a grower, like my Mary. He is saying that the people have asked him to govern the country pending elections. He is saying that Butcher Boy is dead. It didn't happen through a military coup. It didn't happen through civil uprising. Butcher Boy died of a cardiac arrest in very salacious circumstances. Apparently he'd had one of his orgies at the presidential mansion with some prostitutes flown in for the night – in an attempt to spread his sexual largesse to other countries – had used Viagra and had a heart attack that so much surprised him that he died. There was also some story about him being fed a poisoned apple by one of the prostitutes. In any case, Nigeria was now free of Butcher Boy. All the poets were going to be released from prison. The dissidents, the journalists and newscasters, even some members of the army who had not seen eye to eye with Butcher Boy and were expecting a death sentence – they were all given a general amnesty and released from prison. And – I can hardly believe it! – my dead but alive-in-me friend, the poet who was hanged, has been given a presidential pardon. And Deaconess! Our Deaconess, has been made Minister of

Women's Affairs. She's on the TV beaming loudly. She's saying something about toasting Butcher Boy with…

"I want to go out on the streets and celebrate! Did you hear that the UN has lifted the ban on Nigeria? And so soon! Let's go out and celebrate!"

My husband is game, so we make sure our daughter is safely with Nurse and I climb heavily into the car, my husband at the wheel.

"I still can't believe it!" I shout.

I wonder if I should feel sorry about the death of a dictator, a man who was responsible for thousands of deaths including the death of my beloved poet friend. It was his death that gave me the beginning for my novel. Now the novel has ended – at least I think it has – all the seven have been taken care of one way or another. I've turned seven right round, I have. Some of my characters are dead and some are alive. I even had Auntie Lou kill the Governor by remote control. She got a mouse and did some things to it of a carving knife nature which I shall not repeat. Let's just say the Governor was unable to urinate on the ship back to England, got bloated and died.

We drive from Ikoyi and Victoria Island with their green lawns, their fences, walls and hedges of frangipani trees, their gardens with croton leaves spiking upward, and the elegant sprawl of bungalows. The clean and neat streets are unusually silent. The elite, guarded by mallams, are silent.

"It's so very weird," I say, and my husband, thoughtful, nods.

We pass the third mainland bridge with its overhead directions to Yaba, Obalende, white letters on a green background, and take the route to Yaba. Even before we come to Yaba proper, there is an acrid smell of burning tyres which penetrates the air-conditioned confines of our car.

My husband says, "Maybe we shouldn't have come. It really isn't safe yet. I should have left you at home. We haven't been officially released from house arrest."

"Well, we're here now. It's not the same as seeing it on TV. This is the real thing."

He glances at me. "You seem to be calmer, somehow. Is it because you have finished writing the novel? Or is it because Butcher Boy is dead?"

I tell him I don't know, that I'm not sure whether I've finished writing… I'm not even sure if, as Christians, we should be celebrating the death of an evil person. Does Judas Iscariot, who sold Christ into death, which resulted in our life, does he deserve our pity as he rushed to the field of blood and hanged himself?

"The characters in my novel… You know I love them as if they are my own children. Even the evil McTurkeyen and the Governor. I wish I could have somehow indicated that to those two in particular."

"Well, you're the writer. What did you do with them?"

"I had Auntie Lou, you know the midwife who plotted a failed slave revolt with…"

"You wrote a novel about slavery in nineteenth-century Demerara, your own country, and you, a black woman, a descendant of slaves, you had the slaves revolt against the whites and then made the slaves fail?"

"I'm not sure that they failed. Some of them wanted to do their own thing and I let them."

Our conversation comes to a halt just as a band of youths, their heads happy-highed, with strips of cloth wound round their waists, approach the car. One swigs from a bottle. They have made an effigy of Butcher Boy. His body is sackcloth, his blood is sawdust pumped into arms and legs and he is suspended from a stick. Around his neck is a rope pulled tight. On his semblance of a face a pair of dark sunglasses are taped. The effigy is propped up against huge drums of kerosene and a burning tyre sears it in flames which lick and consume the body right up to his neck.

"Celebrate with us, I beg!"

A youth shoves the bottle at the glass window on my side. I turn it down and take the bottle from him, pretending to enjoy the burnt singe in my throat. My husband stops the car completely. We cannot go past the effigy and if we are to move we will have to reverse down the road. I've never seen such a thing. Masses of people everywhere. Drumming is heard and the thumping, thwacking, thin-din strikes mix together in a furore of excitement. One woman sidesteps and another lifts her lappa as if it is the arms of a person and does swerving dips up and down, her slippered feet skimming the dusty road.

It seems as if everyone in Lagos has come out to dance. Small boys balance trays on their heads and shout, "Pure water!" I wonder if anywhere in the world there has been so much joy and such an extravagant expression of it when a leader, however evil, has died. Extemporaneous songs are in the making as the fires lick the effigy and as members of the crowd are drawn, like iron filings to a magnet, to leap around the fire, crouching, then jumping. It is a horrifying spectacle. It is a beautiful spectacle.

"What if Butcher Boy repented on his last Viagra breath and we see him in heaven?"

My husband laughs. "I don't think so. I think God has arranged it otherwise."

We seem to be the only ones in a car and the heat from the flaming effigy is making the car like a hot tin box; with the smoke and all I'm beginning to feel sick.

"Let's go home. I've seen enough."

We reverse slowly down the road until the crowd and the effigy becomes just a cluster of undefined shapes. We back into a side road, turn the car in the direction of home.

"Slavery is at an end now," I pronounce. The car skims past the quiet of the houses, the lawns, the trees. The roads are free of soldiers. Any association with the military is taboo today. Those soldiers with any sense have changed into mufti.

"Jesus, it's so weird," I say.

"Don't swear"

"I'm not. I'm being deliberate."

"Don't swear."

So I keep my mouth shut, my thoughts racing forwards and backwards to the Hangman's Game. I have yet to get the full word and the last letter. The novel has ended but I wish desperately to find some way to let my characters know that even as I plotted the stories of their lives, deciding who should smile and when, who should be killed and who should be saved, that...

"I have to admit that I was rather worried about you and that game, especially what you were doing to Nurse."

"What was I doing?"

"You know very well you were terrifying the poor child."

"She's not a child."

He does not want an argument. I'm thinking, though, that I need an argument, that an argument might just cheer me up. It's not as if I didn't give each and every one of my characters some element of choice, some rope. It's not my fault they're ignorant of my love for them. It truly, really isn't. And I'm not about to write myself into their script. It just isn't on.

"Don't upset yourself. Butcher Boy is dead. Our shackles have been removed in a single night by God Himself. We are free."

My husband resolute. His faith alive. Unhanged.

And this is what I write.

Auntie Lou stabs the rat and she cuts off its tail. The Governor writhes. The ship's doctor dips into his black bag and puts some smelling salts to the Governor's nose. The Governor mumbles, "Auntie Lou. I love her... I... If only... If only I could..."

The ship's reverend – a new character – comes in.

"Do you repent?"

The Governor repents. Soppy and...

Never mind. Now for McTurkeyen. Some effort needed. Can't stand the man. He's in delirium with his thoughts of death and murder and rape. I'm going to leave him like that. Enough is enough. They didn't all live happily ever after. I don't feel like changing McTurkeyen's life. I'm not being unchristian. He didn't even tell John that the sentence of hanging had been revoked.

"I've finished the novel," I tell my husband.

"Thank God. Does this mean the Hangman's Game is also finished?"

"No. I'm going to call Nurse and..."

"Come on!" he objects, but he is the one who calls her.

"Madam? Is the baby coming?"

"Yes, in a manner of speaking. What's the last letter in the word I'm thinking of in the Hangman's Game?"

"It's been so long, Madam... I can't remember."

179

I've been counting on that.

"The clue," I declare to her shell-like ears, "is 'Love'." She is suitably silent.

She says "Do you love me, Madam?"

"What?"

I realize I don't love her.

"Do you love me, Madam?"

My husband says, "Of course Madam loves you."

"I don't love you, Nurse," I say, and she starts crying, but just as I'm about to melt she throws herself into my husband's arms. She's done that before. I saw her doing it. Silently I utter a prayer. Dear God, give me the power to love her. She who has caused me and my mind so much pain, she who has tried to hang me. Her fiancé is dead. She deserves some pity; some compassion. Let me love her.

Nothing happens inside me. Absolutely nothing. She's looking at me. My husband is looking at me.

"You're a writer, darling."

"Don't darling me"

"You're an author and you're in the business of creation. If you don't love her, create the love. Just do it."

I try this strategy. Just for kicks, you understand. And I can tell you it needs all the imagination I can muster. I imagine myself loving her and hugging her and, wouldn't you know, I end up doing just that. She's got tears on her face and so have I and I haven't even imagined those tears of forgiveness. Of course, if I were writing a book, my baby would be born at this hour with its metaphorical, symbolic implications. She isn't. But the novel is over and it is finished.

★ ★ ★ ★ ★

It is finished. The last words of Christ on the cross. It is finished. That's the truth of it and we are on the way to the Outreach. Nurse and her necklace with the cross on it – a beautiful necklace that – is at home with our daughter.

It's going to take place at Tafawa Balewa Square in the heart of Lagos.

"I don't want to frighten you, my darling husband, but I'm

going to have this baby daughter of ours at the conclusion of the Outreach."

The car screeches to a halt on the road.

"Let's get going again. You don't have to worry, because I've made arrangements for an ambulance, my doctor, and two of the nurses I like, to be there on standby."

"You've what?"

"Being so involved in my writing, I haven't asked you what you're going to preach about. It isn't by any chance 'The Peace that passeth all understanding' is it?"

"How did you know?" he asks as we move at a leisurely pace along the road. "You're sure? You're sure you want to give birth at the end of the Outreach? It's not the best of places, Tafawa Balewa Square... nor is it the best idea you've ever had."

He's right of course. Tafawa Balewa Square is not the prettiest place in Lagos, to put it mildly. In fact it's an ugly place that the state has attempted to beautify by erecting slabs of concrete from which fountains are supposed to spurt – if there is water flowing, which there usually isn't. Usually on weekdays it's filled chock-a-block with people, crowds buying from the peddlers of every sort who line the roads. Trestle tables loaded with kola nuts, cigarettes and sweets perch precariously over oozing gutters. There are women breastfeeding their infants under faded um-brellas and I note that some have their hair done in long braids, which take ages and ages to plait, but I'm not thinking hanging thoughts – not that kind anyway.

"Why Tafawa Balewa Square and not the hospital... Why couldn't you be less dramatic and have your baby there?"

"It was like a prison for me... that hospital."

"I hope you'll now stop your worrying and, my dear, when you were forever bullying Nurse – well, I was more than a little alarmed."

"Well, if you must know, you really began to irritate me. You kept on saying I should not be anxious about anything, when you could see death all over the place – my friend the poet hanged, the gardener murdered, the thousands upon thousands of men and women given death sentences just so Butcher Boy could stay in power. I mean... really!"

I'm looking at the massing crowds converging on Tafawa Balewa Square; people holding the hands of their children, mostly dressed in simple wrappers and bubas of Ankara – bright bold colours. Some wear sokotos. There is a brisk business selling soft drinks in bottles and cartons from buckets filled with blocks of ice, balanced on heads. It is all a blurred, muzzing haze.

"We'll have to get out and walk, I think… if we're going to be on time. Do you feel up to it?"

He gingerly moves the car near to a trestle table which sports pairs of slippers and shoes. After paying a little boy to look after the vehicle, I purchase a pair of sandals so that I can walk with more comfort.

My husband is holding a briefcase containing his Bible and the sermon; I am holding my stomach with the child soon to be born.

"I want to tell you something."

"Please," he says, "not now."

"Please," I entreat. "Please indulge me. When I was writing the novel, you were always either praying, going to fellowships or planning this Outreach. I wasn't sure you loved me. But I submit. I'll be obedient. I won't say anything more."

"My own darling. Bone of my bone and flesh of my flesh. How can you even think that? But then you were so busy playing the Hangman's Game…"

I realize, when he says that, that I forgot to get the last letter of the word. Too busy loving Nurse. No matter.

"I wanted to ask you if you love me. Do you love me?"

He drops his briefcase with the Bible and his sermon in it. He drops it, drops it where it hangs precariously on the side of a not too clean gutter by the road. A small crowd gathers round for a ringside treat.

"I adore you."

"I know, but do you love me?"

His eyes are astonished and he holds me in an embrace that covers my child, our child, and right there in the road beside the gutter he kisses me fully on the mouth, and the Bible with all of its words and the sermon with all its words are made flesh and I feel as if my once-coffined heart is bleeding alive when he announces to delighted ears that he loves me.

182

"I love her more than my life," he says. Then he bends, retrieves the briefcase with the Bible and the sermon, dusts off his white agbada.

He walks ahead, me tripping after him, between the crowds, in new feet clad in new shoes, walking as Quamina might have walked, as Rosita, as Auntie Lou and the Governor might have walked – without running; as Captain McTurkeyen might have walked.

At last we manage to pick our way to Tafawa Balewa Square. Earlier on in the day, the people from our church had gone before us and set up a stage. Praise songs to God are already being sung and well, let's just say I'm glad God is in favour of a joyful noise.

The organist's head swings to the thumping chime of the chorus. The leader of the choir, a thin reed of a man wearing a dansiki of blue brocade, shouts, "If you see my mother, tell her say, I dey with Jesus, tell her say, if you see my sister tell her say…"

He goes through every possible relative he might have. Aunties, uncles, cousins, grandfathers and so on during the course of the song. Then, after the solemn praise hymn, my husband, me sitting beside him, takes the microphone.

"…That is why there is no need to fear… There are approximately three hundred and sixty-five admonitions against fear in the Bible, which corresponds with the number of days in the year … Our late President terrorized many in this land but… Fear not. Many countries have suffered atrocities like we have in Nigeria," says my husband, "and have taken things into their own hands and revolted. In Nigeria, God's own country, we waited, we prayed to God to save us and He has…"

Then my waters break; my husband has seen the gathering of water on my dress, seen my pain. There is pain and he continues speaking and I submit to it as it enters through my toes and runs pell-mell in a lingering stretch up my thighs. My baby is coming. The hospital staff surround me in a circle. But what dominates my concerns is the thought that I have yet to complete the entirety of the World-Word in a real way, reach the L, the last letter of the word in the Hangman's Game.

I desperately need this "control" and yet my husband's voice is going on when he knows I am about to give birth. He's just going on with his preaching.

The face of the doctor who lifts me up and carries me to the waiting ambulance is not the face of my usual doctor – who is a Nigerian, short with kind eyes, head covered with a tight cap of baldness. He delivered my first child and I had made specific arrangements for him to be here at the Outreach. He, albeit reluctantly, had agreed. Where is he? What trick of fate is responsible for his absence? After so many ins and outs of hospital, am I threatened with a miscarriage, another miss? Another miscarriage of justice such as happened to my poor dead poet friend? Such as happened to John? No. There was no miscarriage for either of them. No. Yes. Have I been wrong all along when I so much craved…?

The pain is excruciating. The doctor shouts at the nurses in the ambulance. Concerned onlookers are told to leave. This is a miscarriage of physical, mental and spiritual justice. Three in one. Isn't that how it goes? To have reached so far, to have finished my novel, to have rid myself of imaginations and fears, am I now to bear this cross? A miscarriage of everything I hold dear? Without… Outside of with. Without a chance to sing magnificats?

He is an oyinbo expatriate doctor. A white man. Sweat pours from his face as he straps me to the birthing chair.

So I'm strapped in. I can hear my husband's voice, microphone-loud, coming wave after wave into the ambulance, like the waves of the Demerara river sea-sawing at the edges of my heart.

The oyinbo doctor is washing his hands. He has wide handlebar whiskers and he introduces himself as Captain. Captain who? Captain of what? How can a captain be a doctor? A doctor? A captain? He fills a syringe ready for plunging the needle into my vein.

"Who, who, are you?" I ask, struggling through the pain.

"Why I'm Dr McTurkeyen."

"No!" My screams cause the nurses to rush to the ambulance. The oyinbo doctor closes the doors. My husband. The baby born. The baby in my husband's arms. She is silent.

"I, I thought one of, I mean, my characters…!"

"The doctor said you were hallucinating…"

"Who is he?"

"Would it help if you asked him yourself? Sweetheart, it is finished."

"It is finished," says the doctor, echoing the words of my husband.

He has a piece of paper in his hand. "This drawing… I saw it and I took the liberty."

He took the liberty. They still haven't shown me the baby.

"I could have sworn that one of my characters, the evil McTurkeyen, I mean… when I was writing my novel I couldn't see his replica in Nigeria, I …"

"It is finished."

We stare into each others' eyes as he twirls his wide handlebar whiskers. I think I want to die.

My husband has a strained look on his face. He walks out of the ambulance with our baby.

"Where did you find it? Where did you find my drawing?"

"I took the liberty of filling in the last letter. It is L is it not?"

"What, what does the letter L represent?"

"It could be L for love… L for last, L for Light…"

"Have you ever been to Guyana, Demerara?"

"As a matter of fact, yes. I'm Guyanese… Before coming here I…"

And I know that my baby is dead.

And the enormity of what has happened, the enormity of my loss is such that I do not know what to do. The Captain and the doctor, McTurkeyen, spells out the whole word of the Hangman's Game, says it slowly, spells it out, like a mighty cudgel of a blow: C- O- N- T- R- O- L.

He leaves me with my thoughts. Thoughts which jibber-jabber and tell me that my baby is dead and that I shall never recover from this loss and that … these thoughts… these thoughts. Other thoughts challenge. Fight the loss you feel. Fight. Fear not. Act. Put a smile on the face of the hanged man who died for you. Who died and rose from death. Who set you free so that you could live again. Live.

And. And I'm crying. I'm crying at birth. I'm crying at death.

I am smiling at birth. I am smiling at death and at rebirth.
 "It is finished."

Turn the page.
I turn the page.

That is what could have happened. My baby dead and me grieved in sorrow. And me in control.

This is what happened.

McTurkeyen comes into the ambulance as doctor and supplies the last letter of the word in the Hangman's Game. The L, signifying Light, seeing the truth of things.

Then he leaves me with my husband and brand new baby daughter and leaves me with the drawing of the Hangman's Game and the word under it and I teach my daughter her first drawing, her first word and I show her, pointing, show her the drawing like this:

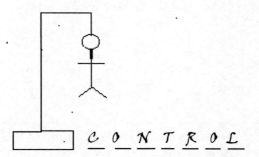

Then I tell her and I tell myself, "It is finished."

Then I put a smile on the face of the hanged man who died for me and rose again on the third day so I could be free and so that I could live again. Then I tell my baby daughter and I tell myself: "It is finished."

THE BEGINNING

ABOUT THE AUTHOR

Karen King-Aribisala was born in Guyana. She has travelled widely, having been educated in Guyana, Barbados, Italy, Nigeria and England. She is now living and working in Nigeria where she is Professor of English in the department of English, University of Lagos, Nigeria. She is a writer of non-fiction and fiction and regarding the latter she has published several short stories and poems in journals such as *Wasafiri, Presence Africaine, The Griot* and *Bim*. Her first collection of short stories, *Our Wife and Other Stories*, won the Best First Book Prize in the Commonwealth Prize (African Region) 1990/91. Her second work, *Kicking Tongues*, is a blending of poetry and prose, in which she transposes Chaucer's Canterbury Tales to modern-day Nigeria. She is the recipient of a number of awards such as two James Mitchner Fellowships for creative writing at the University of Miami, a Ford Foundation Grant and British Council grants.

All Peepal Tree titles are available from the website
www.peepaltreepress.com
with a money back guarantee, secure credit card ordering and fast delivery throughout the world at cost or less.

Peepal Tree Press is celebrated as the home of challenging and inspiring literature from the Caribbean and Black Britain. Visit www.peepaltreepress.com to read sample poems and reviews, discover new authors, established names and access a wealth of information. Subscribe to our mailing list for news of new books and events.

Contact us at:
Peepal Tree Press, 17 King's Avenue, Leeds LS6 1QS, UK
Tel: +44 (0) 113 2451703 E-mail: contact@peepaltreepress.com